THE EARL'S FALCONER

THE
Earl's Falconer

By URSULA MORAY WILLIAMS

Illustrated by Charles Geer

WILLIAM MORROW & COMPANY

New York, 1961

To

the boys at Court Farm House

Acknowledgment

I would like to thank Lieutenant-Colonel N. C. Faithfull for his help in reading and correcting technical points in this book, and to explain that, for the sake of the story, I have occasionally used the exception that proves the rule.

My thanks are also due to the librarians and staff of Gloucestershire and Worcestershire public libraries for untiring help in providing books of reference on falconry.

U. M. W.

Some of the terms used in the art of hawking may be unfamiliar to readers, and the author has therefore supplied a glossary, which appears on pages 187 to 189.

Contents

Contents

CHAPTER 1

The Boy and the Bird

HIGH ABOVE THE FOREST, THE TUMULT OF THE October wind raged between heaven and the upper branches, thrashing the groaning pines, stripping the beech leaves. A hundred feet from the ground, where the branches of a beech and a pine jostled and clawed and sometimes intermingled in the storm, a bird and a boy faced each other across the void. They were swept apart or came together, and looked at one another and avoided one another's eyes.

The bird was a beautiful peregrine falcon,

caught in a notch of the tree by a silver varvel, or ring, attached to her jesses, the leather thongs which usually bound her to the falconer's wrist. Mercifully, she was not hanging, but was a prisoner, unable to fly, perched on the frail, outer branches of the pine.

She had been captured on the plains of Flanders and at first had proudly resisted man's mastery over her. Meeting only affection and patience from her falconer, after a while she suddenly submitted, and became his pride and joy. For three long, bright seasons she obeyed his will, and who knows what primeval urge caused her to fly off that wild October afternoon? Avoiding her quarry, she sailed so far from her mews that her falconer rode seventeen miles in one direction and then in another, calling his own call for her, listening for the faint sound of her bell.

The falcon's heart beat fast now under her feathers tousled by the wind. The sweet breath of freedom was filling her lungs. She braced herself against the wind, straining at her captivity.

When the boughs of the beech tree surged toward her, when the face of the boy opposite loomed nearer and nearer, when the fingers clutching the beech bough began to unclench and steal in her direction, preparing to snatch at her yellow legs, she opened her bill with a short sharp hiss of fear and anger. Reaching out her neck she shrieked, and prepared to fling herself from the bough. At that moment the wind divided the plunging branches, the boy surged down, the falcon was swept aloft, and each was lost from the other's sight in a tangle of leaves and needles. Now they were twenty feet apart.

The boy had never seen the peregrine before. He was no trained falconer, but the son of a yeoman living on an earl's land. Walking in the wood, he had noticed a flurry of birds mobbing a pine tree, while his quick ear caught the chime of high bells, a new note above the autumn wind. Searching and prying, he caught a sudden glimpse of the falcon in her airy prison. He could not climb the pine, so scrambled up the beech and finally found himself at a great height swinging opposite the captive hawk, at times within a hand's grasp of her.

The wind that had raged for twenty-four hours showed no sign of abating. The boy clung as near to the end of the slim branch as he dared. He felt of no more consequence than one of the copper-colored beech leaves that might at any moment be torn off and whirled toward the earth.

When the wind held them apart, he kept his eye on the falcon, to avoid gazing into the depths below. When they approached each other, he measured the distance between them, gathering his courage to snatch and spring. He twined his legs round the branch for safety, trying to relax his clutching fingers, not to think of the long fall, of the ground rushing up to meet him.

Twelve times he was swept toward the falcon, twelve times she hissed and avoided him when he looked into her furious eyes and open spitting bill. Then sickness, which had been threatening, overcame him, combined with great fear and sweating. He dropped his head on his arms, trembling all over. As the branch plunged down, he clung to it with his eyes shut, overcome by a terrible nausea.

Up, up came the bough—he felt the prick of pine needles against his face and knew he was near the falcon. He heard her bells chime in his ears, but could not look; his head was buried in his arms and his chest heaving with sickness. He knew if he raised his head he would fall.

He listened for the falcon's hiss, for her scream of rage, but did not hear them. The pine needles thrashed his head and neck, but still he could not look. Then the bough beneath him dropped like a stone, rising with a sickening swoop as the wind swept it up again. For a few moments he was tossed up and down till all sense of direction left him and he could only tremble and cling and pray not to fall.

Up, up, surged the branch. Once more a flurry of pine needles stung his cheeks and forehead. He opened his eyes briefly and saw the falcon staring almost in his face. Her bill was not open, she was not spitting or screaming, only looking at him with her dark, resentful stare. Her feathers ruffled the moment she caught the gleam of his eye.

He could see the notch where the varvel was trapped behind the falcon. A slash with his knife, he thought, would break the jesses. If he could reach her legs with his left hand, he might be able to release and hold her at the same time. He wondered what her weight would be and what would be her resistance, so little would topple him from the branch into the tossing leaves below. Already in imagination he heard the snapping, smashing flurry of his fall, and sickness returned, blinding him. But with eyes fast closed he found his knife and clutched it.

He resolved in the next lull to retreat by degrees to the trunk of the beech. He felt the branch might snap at any moment and his legs ached with the strain of clinging to it. He resolved to go straight to Adam, the castle falconer, and tell him about the bird. With a ladder she could soon be rescued from the pine tree or, if the wind were still too strong, she would be safe enough for another day. Adam would be only too glad to hear about her.

Better than breaking his own neck, the boy
thought.

The beech branch swept up toward the crown
of the pine, with its awful accompaniment of giddiness, sickness, and fear. The boy closed his eyes
in a kind of desperate trance, and felt the whip-
ping of the needles, the nearness of the bird.

This last blast of wind pinned him against the
pine tree with the might of a great hand. It was
strong enough, he felt, to bind him to his perch as
he lay close by the falcon. For some moments he
was stationary, as motionless as on a rock in the
middle of the sea. All sense of emptiness beneath
him had disappeared. His private terrors, his sickness and giddiness left him suddenly. And the falcon, her eyes half-closed, her head turned from
the wind, braced her lithe, feathered flanks to the
blast and did not care about the boy.

As the murmur of a new gust came roaring and
tearing over the moors, the boy found himself
thrust so close against the falcon that, summoning
all his courage, he put out his left hand and
grasped the jesses. Now he must clasp the branch
with his knees alone as his right hand reached forward to slash the soft leather beneath the peregrine's wildly thrashing wings.

As suddenly as it had come the wind dropped,
and the branch fell away below him. Unbalanced

by the weight of the bird, the boy failed to recapture his hold on the branch that supported him,
clutched at a handful of pine needles that
whipped past his face, swung underneath the
branch, and loosed his knees.

As the bough dropped back he fell like a stone,
down, down, down, a hundred feet down toward
the grass below.

Of all trees, a beech is perhaps the best to fall
out of. Its wide spreading branches, placed one
beneath the other, can do much to break a tumble,
and as the boy crashed and cascaded from one to
another the speed of his fall was lessened.

When he opened his eyes, he found himself
lying on the ground underneath the tree, with the
strange sensation of being completely emptied of
all air. When, cautiously, he took short breaths
and slowly filled his lungs, parts of his body felt
numb and ached on coming to life. He was
scratched and his clothes were torn; he felt
bruised, battered, and rather as if he had been
skinned alive and beaten during the process. But
not a bone was broken, and when he stood on his
feet he only swayed a little.

For a short while he leaned against the beech
bole till full consciousness returned, and with it a
sharp concern for the falcon. He staggered back-

ward to view her, and there she sat in the pine just as before, only he knew she was no longer a prisoner.

Too late to wait for Master Adam to fetch her down. He must manage with the best means he could find before the wild sweet outer air beguiled her. Snatching his kerchief from his throat, the boy Dickon tied a stone in the corner of it and hurled it high in the air. As the kerchief fell, the hawk flashed down upon it and suddenly the drama of the afternoon was over.

To his surprise, the falcon allowed Dickon to pick her up and place her on his wrist, where the jesses, though cut and spoiled, still held her. Then he saw that one of her long wing feathers, her flight feathers, had been broken in her struggling, and immediately his new delight was ruined.

To return a damaged bird to Adam the falconer was risking all his hopes of being apprenticed to his hero. And as if sensing his distress, the bird suddenly threw herself from his wrist, hanging upside down and flapping wildly. Disregarding the pain of her talons, Dickon raised and soothed her as he had seen Adam do, but he had no hood to calm her nerves and shield her from the risks and terrors of the long walk home, and he feared for another damaged feather. Without her flight feathers the peregrine was useless for falconry.

One broken was bad enough, but if more were spoiled. . . .

Dickon became more and more conscious that he should have left the falcon in the pine and brought the falconer to rescue it himself. No one could blame him for a flight feather spoiled by her struggling. But further damage was likely if the bird continued to bate, as the falconers called this wild plunging from the wrist.

Gently he attempted to soothe her, but his strange voice brought such fear upon her that at once she bated again, striking the damaged wing against his thigh. Holding her from him so she could not reach him with her wings, the boy moved slowly to the beech tree and leaned his back against it. Standing on one leg he kicked away his boot and stripped off his sock. With the foot already in holes it was an easy matter to tear one larger with his teeth. Eventually he tore away the complete lower part of the foot.

Having righted the bird, he then knelt on the ground, placed her before him with her back to him, gently holding her between his knees with her wings pressed close to her sides. Over her head he slipped the stocking, drawing it down till her whole body was encased.

Then, cradling her against his breast and crooning to her, he set out for home.

CHAPTER 2

Dickon

WHEN DICKON HAD WALKED A FEW MILES ALONG the road to the castle, he turned aside through a larch spinney, covered a further three or four miles of broken country bordering the river, and came presently to his father's house. All the way he cradled and soothed the anxious falcon, wishing he had titbits in his pocket with which to feed her. She must be hungry after her long fasting, and food might win her heart.

The short October day was closing in. The boy decided to feed and rest the bird before taking her early in the morning to Adam the falconer. It hurt him to part with her so quickly. His own heart beat in sympathy with hers palpitating beneath his fingers in her round warm breast.

As he walked toward the small group of buildings that was his home, a younger boy ran from the shadows to meet him. Dickon stopped. "Halt, Jack! Do not come near me! Be off with you!" he commanded.

"Where have you been? What have you got there?" Jack asked inquisitively. "Is it a bird or a beast in your stocking?"

The older boy pushed past him and entered a tumbledown shed behind the main dwelling. "Be off with you, Jack!" he repeated, but the younger boy only followed closer, while the falcon, startled by the angry tone, struggled feebly inside the stocking. Dickon could feel the striving of her powerful talons piercing the wool. Again his heart throbbed with pity at her distress. "Fetch me a candle then, Jack!" he murmured. "And do not run, but creep. I will show you what I have here."

While the younger boy fled from the hut, Dickon carried the falcon carefully to a far corner, where various objects were carefully arranged on a shelf, or hanging from pegs driven between the wattles.

With a sigh of relief the boy picked up a falcon's

plumed hood and passed it quickly over the bird's head. Hooded, he knew he could calm her, and his relief was so great that he did not fumble or cause the falcon to bob her head aside. He had hooded falcons only rarely before, and then under the guidance of an experienced falconer. He glowed with pleasure over his success, while the bird settled slowly into peace.

When Jack brought the candle, he could hardly contain his shout of surprise at the sight of the beautiful peregrine his brother drew carefully out of the stocking and set on a wooden perch. The broken feather parted finally and fluttered to the ground.

Dickon's face clouded. He picked it up and looked at it.

"Is it the Earl's bird?" the younger boy asked.

This obvious question irritated Dickon. He was now handling a pair of dogskin jesses which hung on a peg. They were new, for he had cut them himself from an old skin given him by the tanner.

"I saw the castle folk setting out yesterday morning to hawk the heron," Jack said. "They returned early when the great wind rose. I did not know they had lost a hawk."

"Nor I," said Dickon shortly. "And I do not know it yet."

"But it *is* my lord's falcon!" said Jack in excite-

ment, his sharp eyes spying the coat of arms engraved on the remaining silver ring attached to the
falcon's jesses. "Do you see that, brother?"

"Ay, I see it," Dickon answered gruffly, stretching and testing the thongs. "It means nothing.
The bird is mine."

"Yours!" said Jack, astonished. "Do you mean
to keep it? But it is death to keep a stolen hawk!"

"I have *not* stolen her!" he retorted. "I found
her maimed."

Jack was suppressed for a moment. The entire
family knew that Dickon thought of nothing but
falconry, and dogged the steps of the castle falconer whenever he could escape from farm work.
They knew, too, that he kept his own furnishings
and fittings for the practice of hawking in this little
tumble-down hut, once the home of his grandfather, a serf who had not yet bought his freedom
from the lord of the castle, a mere peasant, tending the castle pigs.

Old Hog Dickon, who died during the terrible
outbreak of the Black Death, would have been
proud to see his son a freeman—a yeoman who
had sworn fealty to a good lord, and held thirty
rich acres in his own possession, in return for paying certain taxes and giving service to the Earl in
time of war. Proud, too, of his sturdy grandsons,
two of them anxious to improve their lot, the other

so entranced with the art of hawking that the combined forces of father and elder brother could not persuade him to forget this fascination and follow the plough. His father had promised him a goshawk if he would neglect the castle falconry for a few months only and join his brothers working on the land, and in this hope Dickon lived, furnishing his private mews with all the bits and pieces Adam the falconer threw away.

But Jack was not yet silenced. "She is a pretty peregrine," he remarked with a tone of patronage. "I think it is too fine a bird for *you*, brother, even with a damaged wing."

Dickon flushed in the twilight. His brother's gibe had truth in it. It was presumptuous for a boy of his age and rank to dream of owning a peregrine; a sparrow hawk or a kestrel, perhaps, or the odd-tempered, wild goshawk to hunt for the pot. But the noble peregrine was a falcon for earls and grand personages, and the laws were severe on those who aped the manners and habits of their betters.

Dickon kept his temper and asked for a rabbit which the dog had killed that morning. While young Jack went to find it, he surveyed his hooded bird, murmuring gentle words to her.

He fed her with lean portions of raw rabbit, which she ate with hungry haste, and afterwards submitted to the changing of her own jesses for Dickon's new ones. To these he attached a leash which he knotted to the perch.

Proudly he looked at her, full gorged and submissive, decked in his own fittings, perched in his own mews.

"Say nothing to the rest about this bird," he told his brother.

"But why?" said Jack, surprised.

"I would rather surprise Father," Dickon said lamely. "Tomorrow I shall mend her wing and we will see her fly."

"How will you hide the bird?" Jack asked.

"No one comes here," Dickon replied. "Go into the house while I unhood her for the night."

By six o'clock the next morning Dickon was out of bed and had left the house before his father stirred. He hurried to the falcon's hut, half afraid that some disaster might have befallen his bird during the night. But to his joy she was well and seemed calm and rested. She took meat from his fingers and showed no fear when he approached her.

Now came the moment for which he had waited all night, when he donned the buckskin gauntlet, rejected by Adam, now patiently patched and mended, and took the bird on his left wrist. Talking to her, cajoling her, he carried her to the outer air, offering her titbits. Then for nearly an hour they walked together, boy and bird, the boy talking and the bird tranquil, making acquaintance with each other and sealing the bond of trust.

When, in full daylight, he saw her beauty the boy both wondered and feared. Her proud bearing set off the steely sheen of her fine plumage shining in the sun. She must be worth a fortune.

Alden Castle was as famous for its peregrines as for the Earl's training and patronage of the young squires sent into his charge. Because of his noble hawks and his high standard of knightly chivalry, the Earl was constantly asked to undertake the training of the young sons of many mighty houses, both near and far. His wife, the noble Lady Eleanor, gathered around her a bevy of young girls, many of whom had brothers serving as squires and pages in the same household. High among the arts and the culture, both material and spiritual, which were taught the boys, the Earl ranked the art of falconry, with the soaring peregrine as the prince of falcons.

"For so peerless are these birds, and so gentle," he told his knights-to-be, "that no man need fear to imitate them. With the three great gifts of strength and courage and devotion, they serve man, who is their god, even as man should serve his God Who is on high."

The Earl of Alden kept only peregrines in his mews. He would not have his young men trained to fly the short-winged hawk, but encouraged those who had any aptitude to spend long hours with their falcons, under the tutelage of Adam, and of himself, in mastering the art of falconry.

"For the hours they lose at tilting or in sword play, they gain in learning to know themselves in knowing their hawks," the Earl told those who cast a doubting eye at the intensive training of the boys in his castle. "And who shall teach a boy better than his falcon to keep guard of his tongue, to be alert at every moment, to forswear rashness and to study temperance?" So the young knights who left the Castle of Alden to make their way in the world were peers among men, and the Earl's coat of arms on pennon, shield, and halberd was respected or dreaded wherever it was seen.

After an hour's walking Dickon returned the hawk to the hut, setting it in the open now, close beside a stream where no one was likely to notice it. He slipped off the hood and left the falcon to pick at a rabbit's leg. He found his father and both his brothers in a towering rage against him, the elders because Dickon's work had been neglected, and Jack who might have taken his part, sorely indignant at having to do it in his place.

Mucky from the ox pen, he flung the wooden fork at his brother and threatened to tell his secret.

"I'll break your head if you speak of it!" Dickon warned. "Come, Jacky, promise me you will say nothing of it!"

"The Earl will have your ears clipped," Jack muttered angrily. "And I'll not speak up for you. I'll say you vowed to keep the bird."

"Nay, Jack! Listen to me! I do not mean to keep her, not after I have mended her wing. Say nothing till then, and I'll do the work for both of us. I took you to the Michaelmas Fair, Jacky!" Dickon wheedled. "Have you forgotten it? And that I promised you a goshawk?"

The younger boy was mollified. "Father cuffed me for your fault!" he grumbled. Then he said with waking interest, "How can you mend the hawk's wing?"

"You shall see," Dickon promised, seizing an opportunity to win Jack again to his side.

"When will you mend it?"

"In the morning. You can watch if you want to."

Jack laughed. "There'll be little morning left for you. Father has work planned to last you till sundown. You are to clear the stones from Beck's Hollow as we did last May, so that presently Father can plough a new strip there."

Dickon scowled at the hateful task. The stones

in Beck's Hollow lay thick as daisies and for as
many as were cleared away, as many more lay on
the surface. There was no end to such a toil.

"And I am to help you, for swearing at my
father!" Jack added ruefully. "But I have a plan!"
he said, brightening. "In the ditch where we threw
them last time is a great pile of rocks. If we cover
them with new stones to the depth of a man's two
fingers, the pile will be great enough to please
Father, and who shall say how many stones we
have taken from the field and how many remain?"

Dickon marveled at his young brother's wit. In
the kitchen he dodged his father's blows as best
he could and ate the breakfast his mother had
ready for him—home-baked bread and a thick rye
porridge.

He and Jack set out for Beck's Hollow in good
spirits and wasted no time in piling large rocks on
the original pile of stones, till the mound was
large enough to represent a day's labor. This they
covered with earth and moss, and finally a layer
of small stones from the field. Within an hour and
a half they were back at the stream where the
falcon perched. She, having bathed, was drying
her feathers in the sun, preening and shaking herself, and finally crossing her wings over her back.

"See how she rouses and warbles!" Dickon said
proudly, in the falconer's language. The bird

showed no particular fear of the two boys, accept-
ing a titbit and allowing Dickon to take her on his
gloved fist, for he had hidden the gauntlet under
a bramble bush when he left her to her bath. He
hooded her with confidence, leading the way back
to his primitive mews, with Jack trotting at his
heels.

"You must help me, Jack," he said, not without
anxiety. "I shall lay her down on that hay bed,
and you must hold her thus, with your hands
about her body, facing her train. Like that I shall
be free to mend her wing." But the falcon, who
was quiet enough in Dickon's hands, began to
struggle frantically when Jack approached.

"It is the garlic on you!" Dickon cried wrathfully. "Go clean your teeth with a stick and rinse
your mouth! Clean your hands, too, and wash the
smell off you. You will drive her mad with that
stinking weed!"

Young Jack, who had been plucking and chewing the wild garlic that grew on a bank near the
stream, ran away to rid himself of it, while Dickon
soothed his indignant bird and comforted her
with titbits.

When his brother returned, smelling some de-
gree sweeter, the falcon allowed him to hold her
quietly, under Dickon's instructions, while he selected a feather from a small collection hidden
between the plaster and the wattles, and matched

it exactly with the one which was broken. Then, gently spreading the wing, he cut the damaged feather obliquely, just below the break, and did the same to the new feather, so that when the ends were matched together it was exactly the same length as the old one had been.

"But how will you join them?" Jack asked curiously.

"The brine! I have forgotten the needle and the brine!" muttered Dickon.

He ran into the house, to the great astonishment of his mother, who had thought him toiling in the fields, and fetched an earthenware saucer of brine to which he had helped himself the night before from the vat where the pig was salting. From this saucer, with the tips of his fingers, he extricated a needle, about an inch and a half in length and pointed at both ends, the whole length of it filed to a triangular shape with great precision by the smith who made imping needles for Adam the falconer. Dickon had paid for half a dozen of these imping needles for his store, little thinking to use them so soon.

"The bird tries to bite me! Why did you leave me? I nearly let her go!" whined Jack.

"She can do no harm if you hold her as I told you!" Dickon returned.

This task, which he had watched Adam perform with such precision and dexterity and which had seemed so simple, was now formidable, and he hardly trusted his trembling fingers to attempt what should be done.

"Hold her fast!" he warned Jack, thrusting one end of the brine-soaked needle into the lower portion of the feather, to half its length. To his relief, it lay straight down the middle of the pith, ready to receive the butt of the new feather which he now pierced to join it. But inexperience and excitement marred his judgment a little. When joined, the top portion of the feather lay just a fraction to the right, yet so little that Jack could not understand Dickon's dissatisfaction; and when he had wiped away the drop of brine from the shaft, the line of the join could very faintly be discovered.

"It is a fine piece of mending!" said Jack in admiration, but Dickon, who had seen the almost invisible repairs wrought by Adam on his damaged birds, looked doubtful.

"It seems to me the feather does not lie quite true," he said.

"It is true enough! One wing is as good as the other!" said Jack.

"All the same, I will try another feather before the brine rusts the needle and sets it fast," said Dickon.

But Jack protested. He was tired of holding the

bird and she began to struggle. Dickon was forced
to take her from him and feed her to soothe her
indignant feelings. Further operation was impossible; he was afraid of hurting other feathers if she
resisted.

Dismissing Jack, he put her on a perch to rest,
and later carried her for more than an hour, talking to and soothing her in consolation for the out-
rage of the garlic and the pinioning by Jack.

The boys' father was surprised to find them
gone when early in the afternoon he visited Beck's
Hollow. But the pile of stones satisfied him, and
at home Dickon was industriously mending the
oxen's harness, so no fault was found.

"Adam the falconer has lost a hawk," the older
brother said, when they sat at their last meal of
the day. "His boy was asking whether we had seen
anything of it. There is a task for you, Brother
Dickon! The Earl will reward you well for a noble
passage hawk, three seasons old, lost two days
ago in the great gale."

Jack's bright eyes met those of his brother, who
scowled at him.

"Can I look for it, Father?" Dickon pleaded. "I
think I know where it might be!"

"*Might* be!" the older brother sneered. "Aye,
anywhere where work is not, I can guess, and
you'll maybe take a week about the search."

"Yet he did good work on the stones at Beck's Hollow," the father said, suddenly relenting. "And it would please the Earl if he should find the hawk. Well, boy, tomorrow you can look for it in the afternoon."

Dickon could hardly believe his good fortune. Strange to say, his conscience smote him hardly at all. He knew that services rendered to the Earl would advance his father's fortunes, and that his father welcomed an opportunity for such service.

By the morning the brine-steeped needle would be rusting, welding both ends of the feather into one strong spine. A free afternoon would give him the opportunity of returning the falcon to Adam, and oh, if he dared, of flying her first.

Now it was Jack's turn to scowl at his brother's good fortune in gaining half a day's holiday, for when he asked to accompany Dickon, his father merely clouted him on the head. Only the remembrance of the future goshawk kept him silent, and he remained aggrieved throughout the evening.

The family retired to bed at six o'clock, since they rose at dawn and the day closed early in October. Before he retired, Dickon savored the wind. If it blew strongly it would mar his plans. But the autumn night was balmy, and his falcon quiet on her perch. The flight feather, he thought, was well mended, and lay so nearly true with the rest that Adam might not notice it.

The bird pulled happily at the wing of one of his mother's more scrawny hens, which Dickon had shamelessly slaughtered.

CHAPTER 3

The Flight

THE NEXT MORNING DICKON DROVE OUT HIS
father's oxen and toiled till noon, with the sweat
pouring from his face and from the flanks of his
beasts. His thoughts were far from his team, and
he ploughed as ragged a furrow as might be seen
the length and breadth of the Earl's land. For in
imagination he watched, with his head flung back,
a mounting peregrine, circling ever higher into the
blue autumn sky, ready to dive to earth like a
javelin, to kill whatever prey he should flush for
her.

He did not stay for the noonday meal but waited until his father and brothers were in the house. Then he took his hooded falcon and his falconer's bag, and sallied forth with Jack's dog at his heels.

His falcon was hungry, sharp set he called her in terms of falconry, for he knew she would not trouble to kill her prey if her crop were full. Before he gave her up—his new pride, his treasure, he had a longing to fly her that would not be gainsaid, although conscience and common sense forbade it. He knew that he might lose her. But when would such another opportunity come to him, a mere yeoman's son, to cast off a noble peregrine, a true, long-winged falcon, with blood royal coursing in her veins under the dappled feathers of her breast? Quiet and stately, she rode his gauntlet like a queen. Until she had stooped for him he *could* not relinquish her to the Earl's falconer.

He came in sight of the castle, blue-towered in the distance, but turned his steps in another direction. There was no one in sight for a mile on either side of him, but until he had put a thick wood between him and the far turrets of Castle Alden he did not pause, but continued his smooth easy lope toward the moorland country on the other side.

This moor, he knew, was perfect country for

hawking, high-lying, with no thick undergrowth, and having little rise or fall. It was a favorite hawking place for the Earl and his friends, but today it was deserted. A Flemish count, Sir Tormine de la Saxe, had come to the castle with a fine Icelandic gerfalcon, and was flying her in the river sedges against the Alden peregrines.

As the boy stepped out of the wood, an invisible tremor ran through the falcon's feathers. Dickon knew she was ready to fly, and his heart throbbed wildly. Was it a new escape she craved? Or merely the high mounting pleasure of her natural flight? Would she fail him? Would he fail *her?* Pale and serious, there was torment in his face.

With his right hand he unfastened the bag at his waist, feeling inside for the lure which he carried—that bundle of flesh and feathers, the remains of the dead chicken. It was attached to a long line and could be hurled into the air to tempt his bird back to him.

The time had come, the greatest moment of his life, and he was afraid to begin. The calm confidence of the bird on his fist brought back his courage, and speaking kindly to her, he removed the hood. Although his fingers were trembling, this did not frighten her, and her bright eyes roamed the moor in eager pleasure. A new force seemed to possess her strong talons as she roused and spread her wings.

Then, half in agony, half in wild delight, Dickon advanced his fist and threw her off the gauntlet, the light flapping jesses brushing his fingers. With a flash of black-tipped pinions she took the air.

Now, as she circled above his head, he felt he had never before seen or known her. On perch or gauntlet, her whole being seemed to center in her intelligent head and handsome, powerful talons. Aloft, head and talons became secondary to the magnificent power of her soaring wings, so justly called her sails, and her slim, exquisite body.

Small wonder that the boy gasped on freeing her, and the falconer's cry he had prepared froze on his open lips. He gazed upward in awed enchantment. Then panic seized him that she would never return. Each wide circle took her higher. She mounted steadily, like the fine game hawk she was. The thin crying of her silver bells became fainter and fainter, so that fresh agony seared his heart. Taking out the lure on its long line, he flung it wildly into the air.

She saw it, and now a new instrument was made of her flight—if flight it really was—that half closing of the wings, stooping so swiftly toward the earth that in one moment the sky was empty, cleaved by the silver streak that fell, rather than flew, with a chorus of chiming, invisible bells. Seizing the lure, she was no longer a dream of speed and elegance, but a magnificent falcon, anxious for her reward, primitive hunger in her eyes.

The boy was trembling all over with excitement. He walked in quietly and took her up, offering her a titbit so that she might not overgorge upon the lure. She did not object, but not until she sat, rehooded, on his fist, did Dickon cease to tremble. Now he knew he must see her fly at full pitch, to live game, this living thunderbolt, for until he had won the utmost from her he could not find the heart to renounce his stolen claim. He called up Jack's dog and sent him away to find a partridge in the sparse undergrowth.

While the dog quartered the neighboring moorland, boy and hawk waited patiently, the boy's chest still heaving, the falcon scarcely affected by her first short flight.

Everything was very quiet. The dog's paws made a gentle rustling in the drying October grass, and if the quest had been prolonged Dickon might have become aware of far-off footfalls in the wood behind him, or caught the murmur of voices. But before the sounds came traveling on the air the dog paused, rigid, half lowered his head, and fixed all his attention on a low bunch of brambles. As he watched he became even more tense and preoccupied—one paw was raised in the air, while a tremor running the length of his spine to the tip of his tail betrayed his great excitement.

Dickon hoped it was not merely a rabbit, but Jack's dog always yelped for rabbits and now he was extraordinarily quiet. His heart bursting with excitement, Dickon unhooded his falcon, and felt again the ripple of pleasure that ran through her whole body. Again she spread her wings, again the strong talons danced on his fist, ready for flight.

She did not need the beckoning of the wind to tempt her. As his wrist shot forward she took the air, sped this time by the cry that burst from his lungs: "A vol! A vol!" (To the flight! To the flight!)

As she spiraled ever higher and higher, the falcon's circles became wider, with the boy as the pivot of her ascent, and again he had the fear that she would fly too high and never return to him. The castle falconer had told him that the best falcons' highest pitch was beyond the sight of human beings, yet from this tremendous vantage nothing escaped the notice of that dark and vigilant eye. An earth-colored partridge darting to safety from one bush to another, a grouse whirring from a tuft of heather, even the flash of the lure—

any of these was sufficient to bring that living arrow streaking through the air, with so powerful a thrust of its talons that many a game bird died before it realized death had struck.

So Dickon held his breath, but could not stifle his heartbeats, else he might have heard footfalls, closer now, and muffled voices in the wood. Higher and higher the falcon mounted with unhurried ease, and at last, when to the waiting boy below she seemed no larger than a swallow, she checked and soared above him, wings outstretched, her train spread to balance her on the breeze.

His heart thundering now, Dickon walked round to head the dog as he had seen the Earl's falconers do, flushing the hidden partridge down the wind. As he faced the wood three things happened: the covey took to the air with a whirr of wings, the falcon above turned over, half closed her wings into one flat plane, level with her gleaming back, and stooped like a rocket.

The faintly whining bells, the stupendous speed of the flight, seemed to leave the sky shimmering, but before she struck her prey the falcon swooped up above the partridge's head and the fleeing bird dived into another bush. At the same moment three figures emerged from the edge of the wood,

not a hundred yards from where the prey had
taken shelter.

"Missed!" Dickon cried silently, in bitter disappointment, and his fury raged against the
strangers who had startled his bird in her moment
of triumph. While she rose again, circling above
his head, Dickon hurried after the partridge. But
they raced toward him, shouting, and he saw they
wore the livery of Alden Castle. His blood ran
cold and suddenly his cheek was ashy pale.

"Hold! Hold!" the strangers cried, approaching.

Two were boys no bigger than he, the third
almost a young man, of so blond and striking a
beauty that Dickon marked it even in his fear.
This young man wore a falconer's gauntlet upon
his left fist, while one of his companions carried a
bag.

"Hold!" panted the shortest. "If you do not
mean to damage the hawk let the partridge lie!
Do not drive her on to wreck her sails in the trees
or perish in the wood!" So anxious was he that he
seized Dickon by the arm, the trembling arm that
wore the mended doeskin gauntlet.

"The lure, Godfrey! The lure! Fetch her down
to the lure!" the eldest commanded. "Give it to
me from the bag!" The lure was found and handed
out. The tall fair youth took it in his hand, and

walked some distance from the rest, calling a peculiar cry.

The falcon circled uncertainly above them, waiting on at no great height, as if bewildered by the newcomers. She could not see her quarry, and the boy who had flown her was surrounded by a crowd of others. But at the young man's cry she could be seen to check, and to shift her range till she circled above the striding stranger and both were far out on the open moorland.

While the three boys watched, the young man threw the lure, and for the third time Dickon saw the splendid stoop of his borrowed bird till she was lost to sight in the heather. The young falconer waited for a while, watching before he went forward and bent down. Presently they saw he had the falcon on his fist. He was feeding and caressing her.

Dickon's instinct was to slip away unnoticed, but a desire to see the last of his well-loved prisoner, and to know if all was well with her, bound him to the heels of the castle squires as they joined their companion.

"Is all well with her, Edward?" asked one of them.

"All seems well," the young man replied. "I never thought I would see her again. My beautiful!

My proud queen!" he murmured to the falcon. "I never knew such pleasure as when I heard your bells again!"

"She eats well, but retains her grace and dignity. I would not say she is starving for food," remarked the third squire.

"And this is the third day she has been free!" said the other. "She has looked after herself well— or has someone been keeping her?" he added, rounding suddenly on Dickon. "What do you say, lad? How did you come to steal this falcon?"

With all his heart Dickon now wished he had taken to his heels. He was trembling from head to foot. "I did not steal her!" he muttered.

"Did not steal her? Why, by my faith, she is wearing new jesses!" cried the third squire. "Knave and liar! Wait till I give you what you deserve!" He dealt Dickon a clout that the boy's strong arm could scarcely parry. He staggered and nearly fell.

"Peace, Joslyn!" came the deeper, calmer voice of the falcon's master. "Do not judge the boy before he is fairly accused. We have not yet proved his crime."

"If it is not a crime to steal another man's falcon, to cut her jesses and fly her privately, then the Earl is not my patron!" said the squire with some heat. "And is it no crime for a presumptuous serf to fly a peregrine?"

"I am no serf! My father is a freeman holding thirty acres of land!" cried Dickon wrathfully. "We yeoman serve the Earl because we choose to. We are his liege men, not his slaves!"

"For all that—I had not heard that yeomen were allowed to fly the peregrine," said the other insultingly. "Nor even to take and fly another man's falcon."

"I did not know who owned the bird," Dickon muttered, wishing he could find a better answer.

"You say your family swears fealty to the Earl of Alden, yet you do not know his coat of arms?" sneered the squire. "When changing the jesses for your own, how did you not notice the silver varvels, with the Alden peregrines on the one side, the lion of Lentwardine on the other?"

"Of Lentwardine?" said Dickon, bewildered.

"Ay, Edward of Lentwardine, who stands here holding his own true falcon. And for whose sake I'll warrant the Earl will have your life, for stealing a noble game hawk."

Icy shivers passed up and down Dickon's spine. He tensed himself rigidly, to hide his fear. There was nothing he could say, but his teeth chattered with a thousand unuttered excuses.

The young man, Edward of Lentwardine, hav-

ing fed his falcon, hooded her, and walked a few
steps toward the trembling boy. "Where did you
find my hawk?" he asked, in a calm and ordered
voice, a marked contrast to the angry indignation
of his friends.

But Dickon was past all speech. His head spun
round and he feared he might burst into tears.

"Can you speak, lad?" the older man pursued,
not unkindly. But Dickon could not. "Then follow
me to the castle," said Edward of Lentwardine in
a sterner tone. "We will take this matter to the
Earl, and to Adam the falconer. I cannot judge it
here."

At the name of Adam, a last fleeting hope fluttered in the boy's breast. He would never, without
it, have had the strength to drag his steps behind
the squires all the long miles to the castle, where,
he felt sure, his fate would be a dungeon, shortly
followed by death.

But Adam had been his friend in days gone by,
and to Adam he might find the courage to tell the
truth.

CHAPTER 4

Adam the Falconer

THE EARL OF ALDEN TALKED WITH ADAM, HIS FAL-coner, in the grassy courtyard before the mews, where the castle hawks enjoyed the last warm rays of afternoon sunshine, sitting on their blocks like hooded priors and abbesses at their prayers.

Each man carried a hooded hawk on his fist, the falconer's charge being a promising young tiercel, or male peregrine. Captured as an eyas, or nestling, the tiercel was reluctantly submitting to man's command of him. Once he bated violently, and once started, with every feather roused, at the clatter made by an armorer carrying a couple of shields across the far end of the courtyard.

Gently stroking his breast and sides and offering an occasional titbit, the old falconer wooed him even as he talked with his lord, whose favorite falcon dreamed on his fist.

Ten or twelve boys from the castle, youths between fourteen and eighteen years old, came to put their falcons on their perches for the night. The older men watched them.

"I think that Lentwardine will never recover from the loss of his falcon," Adam was saying. "It is a pity, when he is so soon to be a knight, and then to leave us. He has made a pretty flier of little Juno, but she has neither the strength nor the speed of Madam."

"Strange how she went," the Earl said. "It was never the habit of Madam to rake away, yet I have seen a certain wildness come upon her at times. But I think the reason was in the gale that arose before we knew it. Perhaps there was already more disturbance in the upper air than we felt down there in the sedges."

The old falconer nodded at his lord. "It is possible that she could not struggle against that tempest. But in losing Madam we have lost the fairest falcon in our mews. Hugh of Beckford and his bird are downcast," Adam said, as a boy with a round face passed them slowly. "His eyas failed to kill today, missing two ducks at the brook."

The Earl called the boy by name. He turned and made obeisance. He had a young bird on his fist.

"Tell me, how did your eyas fly after the duck today?" the Earl asked.

"Why, my lord, she stooped sluggishly and had no heart in the chase," replied the boy dolefully.

"You are too kind to your hawk," Adam said, handling the bird's body. "She is fat and lazy. When next you fly her after duck, see that she is sharp set, and wash her meat in water to take the richness out of it. Then, when she kills, give her the duck's heart, and let her feed well on her quarry, rather than on the titbits you like to lavish on her night and day." The boy flushed and bowed, removing himself and his bird from his lord's presence with the natural grace which all the pages and squires learned in their life at the castle.

Through an archway leading to the outer walls of the castle a small crowd of boys appeared, clustering round the tall figure of Edward of Lentwardine. With his two companions and Dickon, he became the immediate center of interest of all the young falconers present. Birds on fists, they gathered round the older squire, who made his way straight to the Earl's side, where he knelt on one knee, bowing his head.

"I am glad to see you have your bird again, Edward!" the Earl of Alden said with great pleasure.

The old falconer's rugged face creased in a smile of delight. "You have done well to recapture her," he said, "and in such fine fettle! And yet what is wrong with her sails? There is damage done to that flight feather." Adam's keen eye missed nothing. He had seen the mended flight feather, which lay by a hair's breadth out of line with its fellows.

All the boys and one or two of the professional falconers were now clustered round the Earl, Adam the falconer, and Edward of Lentwardine. They stood at a respectful distance, but did not lose a word of the conversation. To one of these underfalconers Adam now handed his tiercel, before he gently took Madam from Edward's gauntlet, and set her on his own.

Perfectly at home, the bird perched like a queen while the falconer examined her beautiful wings, that extended from her graceful shoulders to the tip of her tail.

"This is more than strange!" the falconer exclaimed. "Someone has made an attempt to imp this feather. Who can have done such a thing?"

Edward of Lentwardine leaned forward as if he could not believe his eyes. In his joy at recovering the falcon in apparent good health, he had not examined her closely. He turned round and stared Dickon in the eyes. "Did you do this?" he asked.

"I did," muttered Dickon.

Adam noticed him for the first time. "John Hodge's Dickon!" he said, surprised, and then repeated the name in tones of such displeasure that again the boy's blood ran cold. "Why did you not bring the bird to *me?*" he demanded.

"Where do you live, lad?" the Earl said curiously.

"By Beck's Hollow, six miles off," Adam replied, seeing the boy was speechless. "His father is my lord's true yeoman, as everyone will bear witness."

"How long have you held the hawk?" the Earl asked more sternly.

"This is the third day, my lord," Dickon replied at last, with a clumsy obeisance.

"And you did not bring it to me!" the Earl said in deep displeasure. "Have you heard that a man is punished the same whether he steals a horse or a hawk? Our noble king himself has decreed he dies for such a thing!"

"Indeed, my lord, I did not steal the falcon!" Dickon replied desperately. "I only mended her sail, as I have seen good Master Adam do. When the young lords found me I was on my way to bring her to the mews, my lord!"

At this the two friends of Edward of Lentwardine stepped forward. "We came upon this lad two leagues from here, my lord, flying the falcon at the partridge on the heath, with a spaniel dog," one of them said.

The Earl questioned Edward of Lentwardine with his eyes, and the young man nodded to confirm the story. "It is true, my lord," he agreed quietly.

"I only wished to see her once in flight!" Dickon babbled in his terror. "Indeed, my lord, I swear I did not mean to keep her!"

All the while Adam's stern gaze never left his face, but now another element crept in—puzzlement and a hint of curiosity. "The lad is crazed for hawks, my lord," he said. "His father has, I believe, promised him a short-winged hawk in the future, and he had learned a certain cleverness with me, as this poor sail bears witness."

The sorrowful tone in which the falconer described his mending of the wing seared Dickon's heart deeper than his previous terror. He had not only stolen a falcon, he had maimed her, and he fell to sobbing bitterly.

"Tell me how you found her!" said the quiet, commanding voice of Edward of Lentwardine.

"It was in the great gale!" Dickon pleaded. "I heard the chime of her bells, and saw her caught fast by the jesses in the crown of a pine tree. I climbed the next tree, a beech, and all afternoon we were swung to and from each other by the storm. In freeing her I fell to the ground. I threw my kerchief up as a lure, and she stooped to it. When I caught her, I saw her flight feather was broken and carried her home in a stocking. It was late and she was starving. I wished to feed and comfort her before bringing her to the castle. In the morning I thought I would earn Master Adam's praise by mending her sail, and I imped the wing with needles I had from the smith at the castle, but she struggled so I could not do it well. Then, when the needle was set fast, I started to bring her home, but the day was bright, and I was tempted to fly her at live game. And, oh, my lord!" said the boy, forgetting his peril in memory of that sunbeam cleaving the sky, "I have never seen bird stoop as this one does—as if heaven had opened suddenly and sent an arrow down to earth!"

At this praise of his beautiful bird, a faint smile of pleasure touched the lips of young Lentwardine, but the old falconer continued to look puzzled and the Earl severe. The two squires were impatient because Dickon's punishment was so long delayed, while the rest of the squires, pages, and falconers pressed forward as far as they dared.

"And what does my liege man John Hodge think of all this?" the Earl of Alden demanded. "Does he dare to risk forfeiting his acres for your miserable skin?"

"He knows nothing about it, my lord," faltered Dickon.

"Then let him be fetched," commanded the Earl. "It is better he should know directly that his son is a knave and a rascal."

A servant was immediately dispatched to fetch John Hodge from his house.

"Take charge of him meanwhile," the Earl told Adam, turning away. "When the hour comes, bring him to me in the Great Hall. I will send for you."

After a word with Lentwardine, Adam returned to the mews with the lost falcon, bidding Dickon follow at his heels. While the young men were bedding and feeding their hawks, Adam took the boy and the falcon into an inner room which was his falconer's office. Here was ranged every kind of equipment with benches for the work required, perches, and blocks.

On one of these blocks the falconer signed to Dickon that he might seat himself, while he re-examined the bird's wing, she pulling at a chicken's leg the while with perfect unconcern.

After a long examination Adam chose a feather from the stock he kept and matched it, even as Dickon had tried to do the day before. Then he pulled out a knife and sharpened the end of the feather.

Without any warning he said suddenly to Dickon, "Come, hold the bird for me."

Astonished, the boy came to his side and did as he was told, even as he had done half a dozen times before.

"Hold her steady, but do not constrain her," Adam said, deftly cutting the imped feather at its base. Then he plunged the sharpened point of the other into the pithy center of the stump and bound the two together with a silken thread. The whole operation was completed so rapidly by those thin strong fingers that Dickon could only blink with admiration.

"That will hold until she moults," Adam said, fondling the falcon. "Nature will mend the damage in her own time. But you are a fool, boy!" the falconer added, in the quiet icy tone that lashed Dickon like rawhide. "There is much about you that might make a good falconer. Your jesses are well cut, and I have seen imping worse done, for all its crudeness. Why throw away your life for a childish whim?"

"Will I die, Adam?" said the boy.

Adam turned away. "I cannot say how my lord

the Earl will view it," he said. "The King says a man shall die who steals a hawk even from his equal, and to this you add the presumption of flying a noble hawk above your station. If Lentwardine would speak for you . . ." the falconer mused. "But I think he is much provoked, for he cherishes his Madam."

At that moment the young man himself entered. "Pardon me, Adam, but I could not leave my lord before," he said, eagerly approaching his falcon. "Why, here is a good repair! I wish I had seen it done! I'll warrant Madam cannot tell one feather from the other! Is nothing else wrong, good Adam, except the one feather? Is she whole in every other part?"

"Sound and whole," said the falconer. "And to tell the truth the first imping was not badly done by this silly knave who thinks and dreams of nothing but falconry, till his back is purple with the bruises his father gives him, trying to drive sense into his stubborn frame."

"He would have done better to practice on his own hawk," the young man said shortly, and there the conversation ended.

Adam and Lentwardine left the office together, with the falcon once more safely riding her master's gauntlet, the leash held fast between his fingers.

Left disconsolate on his prisoner's block, Dickon

watched the activity in the mews through the open doorway. The boys were putting their falcons on their perches for the night, feeding them, and carefully knotting each leash to the perch, with ample room between the hawks to prevent their fighting. Between the squires, giving here a word of advice and there a reprimand, passed Adam the falconer, boys always at his elbow, asking for his aid, hoping for his approval.

Dickon saw him talking to a boy whose hawk was unwell. They carried the bird to another room, and presently the falconer returned to his office for medicine. One shelf was dedicated to small vessels and to bunches of various herbs drying.

Adam took leaves and pounded them in a mortar.

"What is that?" Dickon asked.

"Daisy leaves to cure this illness," said the falconer.

"Will she die?" asked the boy.

"This is the third time you have spoken of death this hour!" said the falconer angrily. "If you think so much about it, muse on your past life and ask yourself if you are worthy to die. What are my hawks to you?"

"If I am going to die, I would still like to know all I can of your hawks while I can hear it!" the boy muttered obstinately, but the falconer only grunted and went on with his medicine.

Dusk was falling and the squires left the hawk house. At first the many-toned little bells kept up a constant whispering as the falcons moved and settled themselves for the night, but presently, their hoods removed, they tucked their heads under their wings and went to sleep.

The falconer's room became more and more shadowy as darkness fell on the courtyard outside. Adam slept there at night, Dickon knew, guarding his falcons, his ear alive to the smallest sound, the tinkling bell of the restless tiercel or the bating of an eyas.

And round him the ghostly company of all his furnishings made different patterns in the twilight: the tufted herbs, the leather thongs, and the skins for cutting them; the leashes and the lures and the gauntlets; the falconer's bag and the parchment on which Adam patiently inscribed the achievements of his hawks. The smell of new leather, raw meat, and the messes Adam mixed for sick hawks hung like an incense on the air, but it did not distress Dickon. He would have liked to live in just such another cell.

CHAPTER 5

The Castle Hall

DICKON SLEPT, LEANING AGAINST THE LEG OF THE falconer's table.

Light steps crossed the mews, and one of the underfalconers, a slight, bearded man, shook him by the shoulder. "You are to follow me to the Great Hall. Your father is come," he said.

Dickon stumbled after him, past the sleeping hawks, across the courtyard brilliant with moonlight, under an archway, through a corridor and an antechamber. The Great Hall was dazzling after the darkness, with torches and a great fire.

At the far end, on a raised dais, the Earl of Alden and some of his household sat over the remains of their meal. Supper was over, and the Earl washed his hands in a bowl of water held by one of the household pages. A second offered him a linen towel.

The others sat at tables lining the walls, trestle tables that even now were being removed. Shadows flickered across the brilliant colors of the banners hanging between the windows and on the shields which reflected the flames of the fire. At the opposite end of the hall thin music came from the gallery where the castle minstrels played.

The whole rich scene made little sense to Dickon, who felt himself part of a dream. But his feet brought him of their own accord to the side of the dais, and he saw the faces of the Earl, of Adam the falconer, of Edward of Lentwardine, of many guests, including the visiting Flemish count, Sir Tormine de la Saxe. Then he saw his father standing below the dais at the Earl's side. Small and frightened beneath his elbow peeped the face of Jack.

When he saw Jack, Dickon knew that this was no dream but that the next few moments would either give him back his life or take it away. The younger boy looked piteously at his brother. He at least had no hope of any mercy for him from this vast assembly of rich people, who had every right to resent the stealing of a noble hawk.

If only he will tell the truth, as I told it to him! Dickon thought, clenching his fists. My father cannot help me now, and if Jack loses his wits, there is no hope for me.

The father looked sorrowfully at his son. There was no anger in his face, only a bitter regret. Flushing, Dickon met the look bravely.

Having wiped his hands, the Earl turned to the yeoman. "And you knew nothing of the falcon that your son has held these three days?"

"Nothing, my lord," said Hodge.

"Yet, by your account, you knew your son had furnishings and all a falconer needs to fly the hawk, and kept them in a hut behind your house?"

"I knew it, my lord."

"But he had never flown a hawk of his own till now?"

"Never, my lord."

"Why not?"

"Our land is newly leased, my lord. There is much work to do upon it. I thought if this boy follows his heart instead of the plough, his head will stay in the clouds and our land will be neglected."

The Earl nodded in approval. "Yet I have yeomen and even serfs who fly the hawk," he said.

"Yes, my lord," Hodge agreed, respectfully. "And I had promised the boy a goshawk in the spring."

The Earl turned sharply toward Dickon. "And in spite of this you would steal another man's falcon?"

The world swam in front of Dickon's eyes. When he opened them young Jack was standing in front of the Earl.

"And you helped your brother to be a knave?" The Earl scowled at him. "Do you know that if one can be punished, so can two, for such an offense?"

"My brother did not steal the falcon!" cried young Jack. "He nearly broke his neck saving it from the tree, and he did no more than comfort it and mend its wing so Master Adam would praise him and make him a falconer at the castle."

Jack's clear treble voice gave such an innocent complexion to the story that a glimmer of amusement crept into the Earl's eyes, and laughter ran down the table. Adam the falconer passed his hand over his mouth, while young Lentwardine was openly smiling.

But the acid tones of Sir Tormine de la Saxe, the Flemish count, broke on the scene with a clipped foreign accent. "A strange falconer to take into the mews, my lord. Already he thinks himself no servant but an equal. In my country we would grind him underfoot, so insolent a dog as that one!"

As the Earl weighed his reply, Lentwardine murmured audibly to Master Adam, "I promise you he flew my falcon like any equal. I never saw the like!"

The Flemish knight noticed the aside, though he barely caught the words. His gerfalcon had triumphed that afternoon and he did not hesitate to flaunt his conceit. "In my country," he murmured, across Master Adam to Edward of Lentwardine, "we fly nobler birds. I do not think even one of your spoiled serfs would dare to cast off an Icelandic falcon, or if he did, there would be no parley in the Great Hall to prove his crime. The owner of the hawk would strike him down faster than the stolen hawk her prey."

Edward paled with anger at the sneer in de la Saxe's voice, but he answered coldly, "Times change, my lord, and we keep abreast of them in Castle Alden."

"Ah—abreast!" sighed the Flemish count. "Then my lord will soon be paying homage to his yeomen. There is no abreast in my country."

But now the Earl called Lentwardine, and his voice was cold, firm, and dispassionate. "Lentwardine, you have heard this lad's story. He has stolen and flown your falcon. This crime merits death. Are you content that he shall die?"

The faces in the hall turned from the Earl to Lentwardine. The tall youth hesitated, pride and a sense of justice wrestling with his normal kindliness. "My lord . . ." he began hesitatingly.

De la Saxe smothered a sound in which contempt was so ill-concealed that half the onlookers strained forward, inwardly urging Lentwardine to revenge the insult. But deliberately the young man's eyes turned first toward the Flemish count and then to the face of his own liege lord. "No, my lord," he said clearly, "if it pleases you, I would rather that he did not die for my falcon."

This time de la Saxe said nothing, but the scornful shrug he gave to his shoulders and the contemptuous expression on his face left no one ignorant of his private feelings.

From that moment Dickon's life was saved, although between the babel of voices and the discussion which arose around him, it was some time before he realized his escape. The question of his punishment was now in the hands of the Earl of Alden and his falconer. Surprisingly, they called for Hodge the yeoman and, while Dickon was escorted back to the falconer's office and told to bed himself down on a bundle of heather, the three men stayed in consultation at the table on the long dais.

When Dickon awoke, the falconer was sleeping beside him on the rough trestle he used for his bed. With the first rays of dawn Adam roused himself. "Be off with you!" he commanded Dickon sternly. "Your father knows the Earl's will. He will tell you what my lord has decided for you. And mark me, lad, do not be too pleased with yourself because you have escaped with your life. You have been a proper fool, boy. Bear this in mind—that you serve a noble lord, who has your welfare much at heart, and to whom you owe not only your life, but all that is best in your hereafter. Do not come to me before I send for you," he added severely.

The falconer's last words persuaded Dickon that he was not banished forever from the castle mews, so turning his back on the delectable tinklings and murmurings of the rousing hawks, he made haste to his home, ready to face with stoical courage whatever punishment had been ordered him by the Earl.

His father was not in the best mood to receive the prodigal. He had been robbed of half his night's sleep. He was greatly concerned for the life and safety of his son, and afraid Dickon's disgrace might bring about his own ruin. Dickon's mother's tears and the queries of his two brothers occupied Dickon's attention for some while after his return. He was driven out to work before he could hear his fate, and the long day passed in a state of apprehension. He could hardly believe his ears when his father told him briefly at sundown what had been planned for his future.

He was to be apprenticed to Adam the falconer, but only when certain conditions had been fulfilled. He was to work, as hard, the Earl had said, as his father could drive him, and at the same time he was to train a goshawk to the requirements of Adam. Both the Earl and Adam knew that every particle of courage and ability in the boy would be strained to the utmost by these twin tasks, but Adam believed he had the instincts of a falconer deeply rooted in him. If he could develop these in mastering the difficult short-winged hawk, both the Earl and his falconer believed that a fine apprentice would be forthcoming.

They had persuaded his rather reluctant father that the boy was likely to do him more credit as a falconer than a farmer. Hodge fully intended to make his son's life as difficult as ever the Earl intended, and to add his own thrashings as opportunity occurred.

CHAPTER 6

The Goshawks

THE INCIDENT HAD CAUSED SOME STIR AT THE castle, particularly among the squires, who took the greatest interest in their hawks. These discussed the subject freely while bathing and airing their peregrines in the morning. They thought Dickon had escaped very lightly.

Some of the squires said that their friend and hero Lentwardine had begged for Dickon's life. He was their pattern of chivalry, the natural head of all the squires, and each new tale told added to his credit. But others pointed out that Master Adam had as keen an eye for a promising falconer as for a game hawk, and it was this same sound judgment which had persuaded the Earl to spare the boy's life.

"I wish him joy of his goshawk," said one boy. "A more unpleasant bird I never encountered."

"Did you speak of goshawks?" asked another. "Do you know that our new squire, the black-browed Gareth from Wales, is under sentence for insolence to Sir Tristram, the Master-at-Arms? Yesterday he fell foul, too, of Master Adam and was discourteous to the Earl himself. Now he stands in Master Adam's office and his brow is as black as a crow's."

"And so you call him a goshawk?" someone asked.

"Ay!" laughed the squire. "But it was Master Adam who named him. I heard it as I was passing by."

The boys turned their eyes toward the window of Adam's office, but nothing could be seen of the drama going on within.

Adam sat on the edge of the trestle that was his bed, while his piercing eyes scrutinized the face of the dark youth standing before him. "And Sir Tristram also charged you with this," he said, "that you purposefully misused your horse, spurred him till he bled and tore his mouth, for the sole reason that he threw you in the tiltyard. This, I believe, is the horse given you by your father, for which you have shown great love during the short time you have been at the castle."

The boy said nothing. His breast rose and fell quickly at the mention of his horse.

"Where you lack courtesy I do not trespass," the falconer continued. "Others can correct you on this matter. You profess to love falconry, which is the pride of this castle. And I have seen you cherish your hawk as fondly as any who wear the gauntlet. But twice I have seen you lose control of that which lies in a man's breast to prove him man or beast, and last evening I truly thought you would kill your hawk."

The youth blanched but remained silent.

"The Earl and I have talked it out," Adam continued. "We want none like you in our hawk houses. We breed the noble peregrine, and have no mind to fly the evil-tempered goshawk." Adam put his face close to the young squire's. "*You* are a goshawk!" he said relentlessly. "The goshawk has courage, but sulks on occasion. Flies strongly, but rebels when out of temper. Has affection, but withholds it for petty spites and malices. Needs more handling," the falconer finished quietly, staring at the boy, "than all the noble hawks that fly for earls and princes."

The youth's lip trembled. "Good Master Adam," he muttered, "it is the devil in me that takes hold on these occasions. I did not mean to hurt my horse, nor to mishandle my tiercel. I swear," the boy added fervently, "that I love my horse and my hawk better than I love myself."

Adam nodded. "Give me your right hand," he said, and taking it gently added, "see how gently I hold it, like this. And then like *this!*" Suddenly he crushed the youth's fingers in such a mighty grip that Gareth expected to hear the bones cracking. He dropped the hand limply to his side as Adam let it go, his face even whiter than before with the shock of the pain.

"That is a man's hand!" said the falconer sternly. "A hand that can as easily break bones as imp a broken feather. That is what a man's hand should be. And a man's heart holds the leash of that hand as I hold the leash of that falcon. If I turn you out of the mews, Sir Tristram will no longer admit you to the lists nor to the tiltyard. There is little for you to do but pack your baggage and ride back to Wales. But I have a remedy that I will try, with my lord's permission. In company with the son of Hodge, the yeoman, you shall train a goshawk and see what that can teach you."

Gareth stumbled out of the office through the empty mews and stood blinking in the sunny courtyard. He knew he was fortunate not to be sent away from the castle, where the laws of chivalry and of the chase were enforced with equal severity. But the disgrace of being reduced to flying a goshawk with a mere yeoman's son instead of training peregrines among his peers weighed so heavily upon him that his heart pounded like the blood in his bruised fingers. Almost it had led him to rude retort and insolence, but just as a rebellious falcon, preparing to bate, would desist in answer to a note in Adam's voice, to a certain touch of his hand, so the angry words had died away on the young man's tongue, leaving him hot-eyed and hurt, but without retort.

"I will send for you," came the cold voice of the falconer, at his elbow.

Gareth left the sunny mews knowing he must renounce his falcon, his horse, and all his companions until Adam's command bade him take up his life anew. He cursed the ungovernable temper that had spoiled his life from childhood on. He turned his back upon his falcon, which he no longer had the right to touch, and ignored the covert glances of his companions. His only wish was to disappear and be forgotten. His life at the castle had been too brief for close friendships, and curiosity rather than sympathy showed in the stares of the other squires.

He hurried through two archways into another sunny court and found his young sister Olwen with a cluster of girls, feeding their doves. The rippled cooing, the fluttering of soft wings, the babble of talk and laughter contrasted sharply with the dignity of the falconers promenading in front of the hawk houses.

Olwen, who had heard that her brother was in ill favor with the Earl, ran to clutch his arm. She wept bitterly when she heard his fate.

"Faith, if I could melt out my tempers with your tears I would not have fallen in so much disgrace," Gareth said angrily. "Go back to your doves! I want a sturdy tree for a sister, not a stream in spate!"

Olwen was turning away when she bumped into Edward of Lentwardine, proceeding through the archway, hawk on fist. Little heeding him in her distress, she sobbed, "To be so dishonored!"

"How dishonored, Gareth?" Lentwardine exclaimed, stopping short. "Are you sent back to Wales?"

"No, Lentwardine," Gareth said bitterly, looking at the ground. "But it seems I am to renounce the noble peregrine and learn to man a goshawk with a yeoman's son."

"And you call that dishonor?" said Lentwardine curiously. "Then you must have a strange kind of pride. What do you know of the goshawk?" he added, sitting on the low wall with his falcon happily sunning her feathers and throwing her hood from one side to the other.

"Only that it is spiteful and uncertain of temper, that it does not soar, but kills from the fist—a cook's bird," muttered Gareth.

"Yet the noblest in the land ride forth with the goshawk on hand," Lentwardine said. "Did you know that?"

"No," Gareth said shortly. "We fly the peregrine in Wales for pleasure and the goshawk for the pot. The Earl has no love for the goshawk; that is why he purposely dishonors me in this manner."

"It is true," Edward said levelly, "that my lord the Earl prefers the noble peregrine above all hawks. But I would say the Earl does not dishonor you, but rather rates you highly in bidding you prove yourself by manning a goshawk. For if you accomplish this well, the Earl will surely honor you. And if I have heard right, a tame goshawk will prove the submission of *two* proud spirits." His eyes were kind though his words were stern.

"But to work with a yeoman's son!" muttered Gareth.

The kindness faded from Edward's eyes. "We are here to learn courtesy and the perfect ways of knighthood," he said. "Anyone who forgets this must be dealt with."

Gareth was instantly subdued. "Maybe you are right, Lentwardine," he said.

"Yes, I *am* right," said Edward. "And why do you scorn a yeoman? If his grandfather was a serf, may his son not be a squire and his grandson a knight, maybe before you win your spurs, Gareth? You would do well to accept humbly the task that has been given you, before you think to rate yourself a gentleman again."

CHAPTER 7

Gareth and Dickon

MANY OF THE AUSTRINGERS, FLIERS OF SHORT-winged hawks, were accustomed to let their goshawks go free in the spring to breed in the woods. Thus their stock was renewed from birds of reputation, and a good supply of hawks was usually to hand. Adam the falconer had not long made known his needs among austringers of his acquaintance before a pair of goshawks was brought to the Great Hall.

This hall was not only the living room of the Earl and his household, but also the center of the whole life of the neighborhood. The poor came there to beg for bread, the sick to ask their Earl's lady for medicines. Merchants brought silks and tapestries, unwrapped them in the outer court, and were invited in to display them to the admiring household in the Great Hall. Wandering entertainers, jugglers, jesters, and mummers were frequent guests. Whole retinues of the Earl's friends and their households lined the trestle tables, ate, drank, and made merry, and were entertained for days in succession.

The young noblewomen being educated in the castle had their looms and spinning wheels concealed behind the hangings of the hall by night, drawn into the open by day, as they gathered round their lady for instruction, or to hear and exchange tales and ballads. Here they learned the housecrafts of the day, and were taught the graces and manners expected of a great lady.

Soon after Gareth had faced Adam in his office, the two goshawks were brought to the Great Hall. The goshawks were much larger than the peregrines, the male being smaller than the female, and the fierce light eyes, the bristling feathers on their reddish-brown bodies, and every scale on their powerful legs witnessed their wild ferocity. Their bills hinted of a cruelty not seen in the true falcons. Strength they had, and a certain magnificence in their captivity, but they lacked all the royal dignity of the peregrines.

Adam the falconer strode into the Great Hall at the same moment as the Earl appeared from his sleeping quarters on an upper floor. Both were angry that the young birds had been thrust unhooded into the noisy crowding of the castle company instead of being quietly conveyed into the mews. The fury and terror of the goshawks were very apparent, although for the past two or three days they had been handled by men. At a word from Adam, the two austringers followed the Earl and his falconer to the hawk houses. Here the goshawks were put into hood to quiet them.

After careful examination Adam found both birds suitable for the boys to handle. The female hawk was a better bird than the tiercel, with a large beak, a large foot, a short tail, and an upright stance which gave her a fine, well-knit appearance. But the tiercel seemed rather sweeter in temper, and was given to Gareth. This grieved and angered him, for he expected first choice of the birds and there was no doubt which was the more handsome hawk.

The Earl and Adam knew what they were doing. Gareth would find his bird exacting enough without any further strain on his temper, while

Dickon, born the more natural handler of hawks, was likely to make better headway with the female. The impatient Welsh squire had it in his favor that he could give almost all his time to taming his hawk, while Dickon's hours must be stolen here and there from working on the farm, and Adam shook his head over the task that lay before the boy.

Dickon, however, was full of enthusiasm when at last he was summoned to the castle and fitted with a gauntlet stout enough to protect him from the fierce talons of his new hawk.

The falconer had fastened a bell to the bird's tail, and new jesses, with a leash, to her legs. She must never be allowed to escape, Adam told the boy, else she would kill other hawks or fly away for good.

Her feeding, bathing, and care were carefully explained. Once each week Dickon was to come to Adam for instruction. He was to handle the hawk every possible minute that he could spare, and at first he was to watch with her and prevent her sleeping for two whole days and nights.

She was not to be starved, but kept at a pitch where food became a means of approaching her. The same instructions were given to Gareth. The boys were standing opposite to Adam in his office, resentful of one another, each determined to make his own bird the better hawk. But where Dickon's heart leapt for pleasure at the weight on his fist, at the thought that here and now his life as an austringer was beginning, the dark-browed Gareth was full of bitterness. He despised the goshawk he carried and mourned the lithe clean lines of the gentle peregrine he had borne so often to the chase.

Gareth took his bird to the hawk house he had been given for its home. Adam had cut both birds' talons lest they should tear the boys' wrists, and even now the young squire felt his arm as a mere twig in the powerful clutch of the bird he carried.

Gareth closed the door. The only light came from a high slit under the roof, but he could see the bird bristling with hate and rebellion, ready to bate the moment he removed the hood.

"Poor devil!" Gareth murmured, mechanically stroking the tiercel with a feather, at which the hawk struck and snapped. "We are in the same case, you and I!"

Hour after hour they must be each other's unwilling companion, one watching the other, going without sleep till the man had proved himself the master and the hawk at last succumbed to his will.

"You hate me!" Gareth murmured to the hawk. "And, by my faith, I hate myself too!" He laughed a mirthless little laugh in the dark hawk house. Their mutual loathing weighed on him like a physical burden, yet, as the bird again thrust its angry bill toward the feather that stroked, but did not caress, a strange sensation rose slowly in his throat, a sensation so physical that he did not know it was sympathy until hot tears pricked behind his eyes. Still hating himself, at that moment a real love awoke within him for his bird and it was from this moment that Gareth began to train his goshawk.

Dickon never forgot the rigors of his first few days and nights as an austringer.

Adam had provided the bird with a good hood. He feared both boy and bird would be completely exhausted if the goshawk were allowed to bate off his glove for the whole of the distance that lay between the castle and Dickon's home. It was nearly dark when he arrived and, in contrast with Gareth, Dickon's heart was already expanded with a great affection as he held the hawk on his fist in his own hawk house and tried to feed her.

At first the goshawk wanted neither his titbits nor his love. With every feather raised she twittered her hate and loathing, bating backward time after time, to hang head downward in senseless fury.

Then the long, long night began. Hour after hour the boy coaxed and tempted her, drawing a chicken's wing across her great feet, rough and scaly from lack of condition. He hoped that she would snap at it and find his offering sweet, but she only spurned and loathed him.

Time after time with aching wrist he raised her, and no lover ever spoke more sweetly to his true love than Dickon to his bird. But each time she flung herself down, twittering and flapping, spurning the mouthfuls he offered, though he guessed she was ravenously hungry. He offered her fresh raw meat, but it might have been paper for all the notice she took of it. Her bill only opened to voice her indignation. When it closed on the meat she spat it out.

After a while she grew tired of biting the stick Dickon used for stroking her head and sides, for it was hard and hurt her bill. But when he discarded it and used his hand, she bated again, and for ten minutes would not sit for one moment upright, but flung herself from her jesses till his arm ached with the weight of her, and his heart with a feeling close to despair.

All of which was guessed by Adam the falconer, six miles off in the castle, unable to sleep through wondering how the night went with his young austringers.

Gareth had never before watched all night with a hawk, for in Wales his father's falconers had undertaken this, the most exacting part of the training. The tiercel was quieter than Dickon's bird, but its stubbornness and spite appalled him. Apparently reconciled at one moment, the next it would fling itself head downward, flapping, shrilly twittering, and resisting every effort to replace it on his wrist. Hour after hour this went on till Gareth's throat was dry of blandishments, and the aching of his arm had passed to a weary numbness.

Then, slowly, the bird began to tire, and as the frantic struggles ceased, the ruffled feathers subsided, and the breathing slowly became normal. Now Gareth too relaxed. He had no idea how much of the night was gone. Unlike Dickon, who could hear the barking of a fox, the chewing of oxen, and the cries of night birds round his father's home, Gareth could hear no sounds of the outside world, for the castle walls shut them all out. Even the small, intimate noises of the household were silenced by several feet of solid stone, and a warren of passages, small courts, and ante-chambers.

Far away a man-at-arms coughed, and someone knocked a lance against a wall, but all Gareth heard was the sigh of the night wind, seeking the corners of the castle, while far above, the slow stars silently planned the progress of the night.

CHAPTER 8

Olwen and Lentwardine

INEVITABLY MORNING ARRIVED. THE FIRST STEADY
footsteps swelled to a noisy bustling as the castle
woke. Hounds bayed, horses neighed, grooms
swore, squires, pages, and falconers came thronging to their business in courtyard and mews.

Hawks were fed and set out on their perches to
enjoy the sunshine. They mantled and roused in
great content, expanding first one wing and then
another, then stretching both upward till they
nearly touched across the back, while the tail
spread out like a fan beneath the rapierlike sails.

Gareth, watching from inside his own hawk house, compared his goshawk unfavorably with the beautiful birds outside. Large it was and bold, possessed even of a certain dignity, but its short wings and long tail demeaned it, thought Gareth, and now that it sat quiet, exhausted and sleepy, he despised it with all his heart.

Master Adam came up to help him feed it. All through the night Gareth had offered titbits through the hood, tapping the resentful bill with scraps of lean meat, and stuffing them inside when the angry bird snapped at him. Lately the goshawk had accepted them, and the carefully measured portion brought by the master falconer was well received. Adam then left the squire a rabbit's leg at which the bird could pull to keep him occupied.

Adam read the fatigue and boredom written on the white face of the squire. "It is not enough to keep your bird awake, you must interest and entertain him!" the old falconer urged. "A bored and sulky hawk is slow to be manned and you would not watch a *third* night with him, would you?"

"Not I!" cried Gareth hastily.

Adam smiled. "Walk him out presently, keeping at a distance from anything that may frighten him," he advised. "Take him near the horses, and within hearing of the ladies' courtyard, for their voices and cries are sweet to the ear. If he shows too great a fear, comfort him and bring him back into the darkness. I think you are fortunate in your bird, for as a goshawk he seems more kindly by nature than most of that breed."

Gareth, thinking of the frantic struggles of the long night, laughed shortly, murmuring that hawk and man alike were at their best when full of meat. But at the thought of spending another night alone with the goshawk, sweat broke out on his brow.

The old falconer seemed to read his thoughts. "It would be as well for you and for your hawk if you found someone to help you watch tonight," he said thoughtfully. "Have you a friend that would carry the bird for an hour? Of course no one but you should feed it."

Gareth cast down his eyes and muttered something about having come so recently to the castle that he knew no one. He was well aware that he had no friends, and could think of no one who would willingly give up a night's sleep to do him a favor. His sharp tongue, hot temper, and rough ways had not endeared him to the other squires.

Even his little sister was afraid of him. But she came to him soon, asking him if he were not tired unto death, and whether Adam would not allow him to put the bird down this night and go to bed.

"Ay, if I can find a friend to watch for me!" Gareth sneered. "He knows I have no friend. Why did he not promise to send me one of the falconers?"

"I will carry the bird for you!" Olwen cried.

For the moment the hawk seemed quiet enough, pulling at his rabbit's leg with sullen greed. He could not see Olwen through the soft hood and strangely enough her voice had not disturbed him. But in the sudden unwarranted manner of goshawks, all in a moment he flung the leg from him, plunged headlong from Gareth's wrist, and hung by the jesses twittering shrilly and thrashing his wings.

Olwen leaped backward into the courtyard in terror. She had been peeping round the door into the darkened house.

"So much for your carrying him tonight," Gareth said ungratefully, having restored the flapping bird to his aching arm. "Go back to your harp and your embroidery!"

Olwen ran back to the ladies' quarters with an aching heart. Her brother was unkind, but he had looked so tired. How could he watch another whole night with that terrible monster? It was a wonder his arm was not broken by its passions.

If the Lady Eleanor noticed Olwen's tears as

she taught tapestry stitches to the girls in the Great Hall that morning, she said nothing. Olwen's friend and sewing companion, young Lady Catherine of Winchester, noticed her sadness however, and when the Earl's wife had turned aside she whispered, "What has happened?"

"My lord has been so hard on my poor brother!" Olwen whispered. "All the night long he has fought with a cruel, untamed beast, and today he must toil till nightfall with the same hateful bird, and yet again tonight—till strong as he is I am afraid the bird will tear him to pieces!"

Catherine shivered at the picture. "Is the bird so large and strong?" she asked.

"Oh, a terrible size!" Olwen said. "It has legs like a crane! And a great snapping beak like an eagle that raves and tears—my brother's sleeve is all rent!"

"And must he carry *that* all another night?" asked Catherine.

"Why, if he sets it down for one moment it yells and screams when he takes it up, or flings itself from the perch as if it would kill itself, as indeed I wish it would!" said Olwen viciously. "But tonight Master Adam says Gareth may share his watch with a friend, only my poor brother has no friends. Oh, why cannot Master Adam send him an underfalconer?"

"Why do you not ask him to send one?" suggested Catherine.

"Oh, I am in bad favor with Master Adam," said Olwen. "Twice he has caught me in the peregrine mews and scolded me for it."

"Why do you not ask Edward of Lentwardine to help your brother?" asked Catherine.

"Ask him *what?*" said Olwen, stupefied.

"Why, ask him to direct Master Adam to send a falconer tonight who will carry the bird an hour or so, just long enough for a man to sleep!" said Catherine. "You would not be afraid to speak to him, would you?"

At that moment Lady Eleanor separated the two chattering girls and Olwen was left alone with her thoughts.

The day passed too quickly for brother and sister. Gareth's bird seemed as unruly as ever, yet at least there was comfort in watching by daylight, and in the company, distant as it was, of his fellow squires.

Master Adam was in and out with a word of direction or advice. He took the bird from Gareth and walked with it a quarter of an hour or more, during which time the angry feathers subsided, the stiff neck relaxed, and the bird's head cocked to one side in appreciation of the expert touch of the falconer's hand.

"He is improving," Adam said. "Already he is used to the hood. In two days you can begin to carry him unhooded."

Gareth dreaded the coming of the night.

"When you are made knight," the young pages were always told, "you will keep vigil all night in the chapel beside your sword and armor." How shall we keep awake? the young boys wondered. Shall we be afraid? Will the night seem very long? But what was a night spent quietly in a chapel, Gareth thought, compared to forty-eight hours watching a screaming hawk?

Olwen, too, dreaded the night. All through the day she tried to summon the courage to beseech Edward of Lentwardine on her brother's behalf, but though she saw him once or twice her heart misgave her. Presently she retired to bed with the other ladies of the castle, the words still unspoken. But Olwen could not sleep, and at last she slipped out of bed, wrapped a long cloak about her shoulders, and pushed her feet into slippers.

She stole out of the room and down the narrow stone stairs to the hall.

Olwen had been brought up from childhood in Castle Alden. She had romped and played in every corridor and courtyard since she was first able to walk. She knew how to avoid the watchmen and men-at-arms who guarded the private chambers; how to dodge the servants sleeping in the hall, and to find her way through the many apartments and courtyards to the hawk houses on the south side of the castle.

She flitted across the grass in her long robe like a pale moth or a small, harmless ghost and, turning the corner, came upon Edward of Lentwardine standing silently beside the empty blocks where in daylight the falcons bathed and sunned themselves.

As head of the squires, Lentwardine felt a keen responsibility for the boys beneath him, a sense that did not diminish as his knighthood approached. He was well aware of the strain Gareth was enduring. He knew most boys would have been allowed to watch in company, or with the help of an underfalconer, so that they might snatch a few hours' needed rest and sleep. Lentwardine had left his bed to see how the boy was coping with his task, and was musing whether to help him in his vigil or merely to speak a kind word and pass by.

He was astonished to see Olwen in the half-moonlight.

"Oh, sir!" cried Olwen, startled.

"Do not be afraid, little maiden!" Lentwardine said gently. "It is Lady Olwen, is it not? And it is your brother who watches his goshawk over there? Did you come to find how he fared?"

"I know it can only go badly with him!" said Olwen, bursting into tears. "This is the second night he has been watching, and my brother is so weary and so alone! One night would be enough punishment! My brother's temper is hot, but he is noble and brave, only no one understands him here. They think him proud and worthless, and that is the reason they degrade him so!"

"Not worthless, I think," said Lentwardine, "or my lord would hardly take so much trouble with him. How would you mend your brother's temper, maiden?"

"Why, I do not know!" Olwen faltered. "By kindness, I think, and with great patience."

"Then call his temper his goshawk!" said Lentwardine. "This he must master, too, by great patience and kindness. You may be sure my lord the Earl acts with much forethought and out of real kindness for your brother. Would it not be easier to send him away from the castle, as we send a screaming eyas? Have you come to see your brother?" said the squire, stepping back to clear the path for her.

"It can do no good, he will be so angry with

me!" said Olwen. "If only he had a friend to watch for him part of this cruelly long night! But Gareth has no friend."

The tall squire smiled in the darkness. "Go back to your apartment, sweet lady!" he said. "Let no man say he is without a friend in Castle Alden. I will hold your brother's bird." And leaving Olwen speechless, he strode off to the hawk houses.

CHAPTER 9

Meg the Goshawk

THE DAYS THAT DRAGGED FOR GARETH HAD PROVED a mingled joy and torment for Dickon. He ached all over from his father's thrashings, to which his older brother had added his own measure of kicks and blows. But the hawk that bated on his bruised arm was his own property to make or mar, this time openly, like a true austringer. This gave him great heart.

His hawk might fight and defy him, might bate twenty times and sulk and mope by turns; every task to be done for his father meant hours of training lost as the goshawk waited idle or dozed on the perch; yet Dickon never lost confidence that some day he would teach her to love and obey him.

The nights, by contrast with the days, were peace, for there was no outside work to be done, and Dickon dreaded the coming of the dawn. Snatching at his breakfast brought by Jack, he fed his hawk before going out to plough. Dickon then left her to weather out of doors, hopefully believing that some progress had been made during the night. But when next he took her up, she raved as if she had never seen him before. But she raved a little less each day, until at last permission came to carry her to show Master Adam at the castle, with her hood removed. She bated only three times in the whole six miles.

That night, with the falconer's approval, the bird slept on a perch in the brothers' room, to the delighted terror of Jack. Dickon enjoyed his first eight hours of unbroken slumber for nearly a week. The battle was won. When he realized his bird could be as gentle as she was passionate, Dickon was no longer disheartened by her rages, and only distressed when she fought him, for he came to love her dearly.

His family took a growing interest in the hawk's progress. Young Jack haunted the hawk house, for he hoped to own the goshawk when Dickon became a proper falconer at the castle, as Jack firmly believed he would.

Dickon's father, who began by believing the goshawk quite beyond his son's power to control, grew daily more impressed, as under Master Adam's directions the great bird became docile and obedient, accustomed to the noises of the farm. She would sit, unhooded, on her block watching the world go by, ready to fly to her master's fist in a moment for the titbit that was sure to come.

Dickon's mother feared the hawk's fierce manners and its size. She thought it would kill her chickens. But she watched with pleasure at its splashing in the bath and felt great pride when Dickon held it aloft on his glove, handling it so fearlessly. The bird was big enough to tear him to pieces, thought the mother.

Slowly the farmer relaxed his discipline and gave Dickon more time to train his goshawk. Because she was no great lady but a common goshawk, Dickon called her Meg. She seemed to know her name, and now she could not see him approaching without striving to get upon his fist. But just when it seemed that the bird was fully manned, a strange and wayward mood came over her, and for nearly a day she seemed unable to bear Dickon's presence, though he exerted all his wiles to calm her.

Deeply hurt at her fickleness, he left the plough to carry her hour after hour, and got beaten for it by his father. But returning to the hawk house later in the evening he found her amiable and fond, feeding sweetly from his fingers and leaping to his arm from every corner of the hawk house.

"Dear Meg! Good Meg!" he told her, comforted. "I did not believe Master Adam when he told me of your moods. I thought I had mastered you for good and all. Shrewish, stubborn Meg!"

All the while he fed her well with mouthfuls of meat, for the old falconer had told him "late feeding at night makes a lusty hawk!" and the titbits he offered her many times a day were only intended to keep her appetite sharp.

Thus, after many weary days, Dickon's goshawk was ready to try with the quarry and Master Adam was coming to help him do it. She appeared keen on the important day when Master Adam was expected, noticing everything that moved in field and furrow, shifting uneasily on Dickon's gauntlet when birds flew overhead or Jack's dog barked in the ditch.

Lately, Master Adam had been so busy in the mews he had scarcely noticed Meg, or so Dickon thought, during his last three visits. He had tersely given his instructions, quickly turning his back on Dickon, so that sometimes he only stayed five minutes at the castle, unnoticed by anyone, and forbidden, because of the fierceness of his bird, to go near the peregrines in the hawk houses.

But the long miles were never tramped in vain. The shrewd eye of Master Adam missed nothing in the bearing of boy or bird, and Dickon carried out to the letter every instruction that was given him.

He had not expected such an honor as a visit from Master Adam. At best he thought one of the underfalconers might be sent out with him to prove the first flight. The whole family were impressed. Dickon's mother cooked a great pie to offer the master falconer for his supper when his business with the hawk was over.

Master Adam came at last. Tonight he was no longer impatient and silent, but friendly and interested. He examined Meg carefully and said Dickon had carried out his orders well; the bird was in fine fettle. She bated once or twice on his fist and Dickon's heart turned over, thinking she was about to begin one of her moods, but Master Adam seemed unconcerned.

"Do you always wash your hands before you feed her?" he asked.

"Ay, Master Adam."

"And do you gorge her three times a week on fresh meat of different kinds, and on other days give her beakfuls that keep her lively?"

"I do, Master Adam."

"And bathe her every third day, with little meat, and give her a cony's foot to pull at, or the wing of a bird to play with, to give her pleasure and to improve her muscles?"

"I do, Master Adam."

"And I can read here that you do!" the falconer said. "I can read it in her bright eye and her shining legs that were dark and rough when first you held her. And though she bates now, loving me less than she loves you, she does not gape or pant afterwards, nor lose her breath. And I have seen her eye the world around her as a right good hawk ought to do," Master Adam continued. "How did she take her fowl last night?"

"Like lightning she struck it dead!" said Dickon proudly.

"Then we will see her with a partridge!" said the falconer. "Have you a good dog?"

Young Jack now came forward with his dog on a leash. All day long he had been beseeching Dickon to allow him to share Meg's first adventure, and all day Dickon had put him off with first one excuse and then another. "If Master Adam asks for the dog you may come!" he had conceded, and the moment had arrived.

Jack's face was a mixture of triumph and apprehension. What if Master Adam were of a different mind than Dickon? But the Earl's falconer said, "Keep the dog behind us, lad!" and all was well.

They walked out half a mile or so to a rough heath. Dickon found his arm trembling, and wondered whether the vibration that seemed to penetrate his whole body came from Meg's excitement or his own. The goshawk swayed on his arm. Her legs like great springs seemed to swing her body. The short strong wings lay close to her sides, her keen eyes followed every movement in the sedges. Once or twice she bated, for spite, he thought, for she had no heart in it. Indeed her mood seemed as enthusiastic and as wary as his own.

Adam halted. "Unleash the dog!" he ordered quietly.

Jack slipped the dog free. At once it ran forward and began quartering the ground, the falconer following, with Dickon at his side. Suddenly, thirty yards ahead, the dog marked a partridge. Tense and expectant, he stood behind a tuft of grass, one paw raised, a faint tremor running down his tail.

The party closed in on him. Up flew the par-

tridge with a whirr, flying low over the brushwood
with a creaking rattle of wings.

At the falconer's command, Dickon cast off the
hawk from his gauntlet, and such was the excitement in his breast that the great cry of falconry
rose in his throat—*A vol.* But because he was only
casting off a goshawk and not a noble falcon the
cry died there, and instead there rose to his lips
a sharp and excited yelp that he used thereafter
each time he speeded Meg after her quarry. She
took it fair and true, and before the flying bird
knew that death was in the air, twin talons seized
it and life departed like the crack of the whip.

"Go quietly in upon her while she feeds and tie
this leash to her varvels," Adam told Dickon, "or
she may carry off her prey and lead us a pretty
dance every time she kills."

Meg made no protest, being greedy to eat her
prize, and once she was secured, Adam showed
the boys which parts of the bird she might be
given to feast upon. Watching her eating, proud
and happy, Dickon felt himself at last a true
austringer.

"She is well pleased with herself!" Adam said.
"Keep her keen! The hawk that flies for pleasure is
worth two that fly for the belly. Fly her again in
two days and again the day after," he added. "And

on the fourth evening come to the castle and we will match the hawks against one another."

Dickon had been so absorbed in the manning of his own bird that he had quite forgotten a second hawk was being trained by the young Welsh squire Gareth. His own visits to the castle were brief, and Gareth had gone out of his way to avoid the yeoman's son.

CHAPTER 10

Meg and Vampire

MEANWHILE, WHEN GARETH HAD MANNED HIS GOS-
hawk Vampire to the falconer's satisfaction, he was
allowed to return to the company of the other
squires and the peregrines. By this time, boy and
hawk had learned a certain affection for one another. But their natures were too alike for complete sympathy, and their hot blood and fiery
temper irritated one another. Although Gareth
had learned much self-control and mastery of his
passions, he fretted to handle the gentle peregrines again, to throw off forever the weight of
the moody bird that perched day in, day out, on

his arm, and which he sometimes felt would be with him forever.

But suddenly he was released, with orders to man his hawk only for a time every day, while for the rest it was put into the care of one of the castle servants—and gladly, blithely, Gareth returned to the old routine.

Once or twice a week he and the austringer servant took the hawk into the woods to keep him in training, but Gareth took no pleasure in it and the hawk had little success. The servant overfed him, to quiet his tempers, and the result was a certain dullness of eye and sluggish flight, and a breathlessness after the chase that Gareth noticed but to which he paid no heed.

Flying his own peregrine, he hoped in time to shed his allegiance to the goshawk. So he was startled one morning when Master Adam told him to look to his hawk that day, for Dickon would match his Meg against Vampire before sundown that night.

Once free from duties in the castle, Gareth hurried to the goshawk's house. The servant had given titbits to the bird and left him to weather on a stump, but Vampire was bored, since little of the everyday bustle of the castle could be seen from his corner.

Gareth unleashed him and called him off the

perch to his fist. The bird came halfheartedly, and
showed no particular pleasure at seeing his
master. His feathers did not puff and swell; he sat
stolidly looking out at the green grass when he
had eaten the titbit Gareth gave him.

Gareth was furious with the austringer, with the
bird, with Master Adam himself. He could have
warned me days ago! he thought, aggrieved, and
cursed the servant for overfilling the bird so early
in the day, when tonight of all nights he needed to
be in perfect condition. But in condition Vampire
assuredly was not.

"Not that there is much to fear," Gareth consoled himself. "For if the yeoman's son has taken
all this while, as Master Adam says he has, to man
his bird, then my Vampire will beat him in every
flight."

Nevertheless, he watched his goshawk carefully
till evening, giving him no food and hoping for
the best. Above all he hoped that Lentwardine,
who had shown him so friendly an interest since
he shared his watch that weary night, might not
hear of the contest and come to watch it. Edward
of Lentwardine did not come; but the boys, carrying their hawks, were scarcely met at the spot
appointed by Adam when the tall figure of the
Earl, accompanied by his falconer, appeared on
the scene.

Gareth paled as he made obeisance to his lord.

Dickon, too, bent the knee, peasant fashion, his heart beating as he thought of their last encounter.

"By my faith," Gareth swore inwardly, "I did not think that it was so great an occasion. Curses on the blockhead who spoiled my bird!"

Having had great success on the previous afternoon with his peregrine falcon, Gareth had recovered long-lost confidence and pleasure, and now to have it dashed by the perverseness of an overfed goshawk was bitter gall. He stared at Dickon, neither proudly nor with particular friendship, but on catching his eye Gareth recognized there the same trepidation within. A half-smile flashed between them and their hearts warmed toward one another.

But the Earl had not come to watch a match. He knew well enough just what Gareth had gained and lost during his ordeal, and that he would never give his heart to anything less than the noble falcon—the Earl's own true delight. So it did not surprise him or his falconer to find the male goshawk rather neglected and moody. For the better discipline of Gareth it was their intention to keep the bird throughout the winter, but to free it in spring to breed in the woods.

There was no question that Dickon's was the better bird. Naturally larger than the tiercel, Meg had a stronger beak, more powerful feet, and a shorter and more dashing train. Today her temper was sweet and even, while Vampire showed himself first sulky and then perverse.

He missed the first rabbit put up by the dog and, sailing away, perched on a low branch, too indifferent to come down. When at last he came to the fist he failed to rouse or mantle, and plainly showed he was bored with the whole business and would prefer to go home.

The Earl, Master Adam, Dickon and his goshawk had gone ahead. Gareth heard the short thrilling yelp with which Dickon cast off his bird and wondered if it had killed. Once he would have blamed Master Adam for giving the other boy the better hawk, but now he was honest enough to admit that no one but himself was to blame. He followed them slowly, coaxing and wheedling the hawk, till all of a sudden Vampire's mood changed. His feathers puffed out amiably, his head moved from right to left as if the woods about him appeared agreeable after all, and the ponderous grip of his sullen talons suddenly throbbed with life.

By the time Gareth had reached the others, Vampire was once more all that was pleasant in a goshawk. Meg was feasting on her kill.

At the next flight, Vampire, too, killed his

quarry, and a cheerful atmosphere pervaded the party. But a little later Vampire missed again, and this time refused to return to any call, lure, or blandishment that Gareth could offer. Each time his owner approached, Vampire flew farther away, the dangling jesses causing agony in Gareth's breast, for he feared that they might catch in some branch and be the end of the wayward bird.

Not that it would be so great a loss! thought the squire, viciously swinging the lure for the ninth time. But the pride of ownership kept him following the hawk, who hopped awkwardly from tree to tree as if he enjoyed causing such annoyance and would continue all evening if necessary.

Finally Gareth marked him in a high sycamore, and there Master Adam advised leaving the hawk till nightfall. "Climb up when it is dark and you may take him with no trouble," said the falconer.

For the rest of the evening Gareth was forced to watch Dickon's Meg flying almost without fault, and earning words of praise that meant a great deal when they fell from the lips of the Earl of Alden or his falconer.

The group returned at last to the castle, leaving the servant to mark the tree where Vampire was perched. Because he had not been dismissed by the Earl, Gareth followed his lord the three miles of country which had been covered, walking a step ahead of the yeoman's son and speaking very little when he had finished praising his rival's bird, as was expected of him.

At the castle the Earl bade the boys good night. He said little to Dickon, as if his approval had been notice enough, but he spoke kindly to Gareth. "I think your heart is still with the peregrine, Gareth!" the Earl said, smiling. "Well, be worthy of your falcon! Now go and find your hawk!"

Dismayed, for he had expected this tiresome duty to be left to the servant, Gareth stood watching his lord retreat across the moat till he was lost in the shadows, Adam walking by his side.

"The place is close to the road that runs to my home," said Dickon, at his elbow. "May I climb to fetch the hawk for you?"

Gareth was touched by the boy's pleasant manner, and he was glad of company. It was easier to shed his haughtiness when the Earl and Adam were out of hearing. Mile followed mile, and their conversation became animated as they related their own experiences and difficulties in manning their hawks.

Gareth, who looked back with horror on those lonely days, tempered only by the kindness of Lentwardine, now learned that Dickon's lot had been even harder and far more frustrating, because of the blows and the exacting demands of his father.

The servant sat dozing under the tree with his dog, though it was too dark to see him until they arrived. "The tiercel has not stirred," he mumbled.

"Nor you either, I warrant, you lazy oaf," Gareth remarked.

"Shall I climb for him?" Dickon offered.

Gareth nodded courteously.

Dickon handed his own bird to the servant and sprang like a cat into the lower branches of the tree. They heard him rustling higher and higher above their heads; presently there was silence, then a short scuffle and a throaty note of protest, followed by steady sounds of descent. Dickon's legs swung into their faces. Hanging by one hand he dropped from the lowest branch with Vampire, scarcely ruffled, on his fist firmly held by his jesses.

"That was a clever capture!" said Gareth admiringly.

"I have climbed higher for the same game!" Dickon said, smiling.

They parted, and now Gareth would not let the servant carry his bird, but walked, fondling and talking to it, all the way back to the castle.

CHAPTER 11

The Young Falcon

DICKON'S GOSHAWK MEG PROVED SUCH A HUNTRESS
that the whole family held her in respect. Young
Jack, fervently copying every gesture of his
brother, learned to handle her. The elder brother
spared time to watch her at her rabbiting, while
Dickon's father and mother praised her openly.
There was always food for the pot now, and Meg
cost nothing to feed, since she caught enough for
herself and for the household, too.

Dickon's father knew that the Earl and his falconer had been right about the boy. Dickon's

heart was not in the land, and when one day the farmer was summoned to the castle, he had little doubt what the business would be about. When he returned, he told Dickon that he was to become an apprentice to Adam the falconer in the castle mews.

At last John Hodge was proud of the boy, and his wife was overjoyed. Their son would wear better clothes, mix with young men of noble blood, see fine manners, and learn the ways of chivalry. It was by no means impossible that later on the Earl might make a squire of him, though his grandfather had been a serf.

Jack, who was much attached to Dickon, was consoled by having the custody of the goshawk Meg. Dickon presented Meg to him freely, but not without an inward pang, for the queer-tempered bird with her courage and odd bursts of spirit had become very dear to him.

When the castle walls enfolded him as the newest and youngest servant in the mews, wearing his lord's livery, obedient to his lord's falconer and to every underfalconer or squire, the life at the farm seemed very far away and the gray goshawk part of a dream that he had cast behind him.

So Dickon became a falconer, and learned the pattern of the all-absorbing life within the mews, where every falcon and tiercel took on a personality of its own, as varied as that of their masters. Freshly caught birds were trained and handled there, and young squires promoted from pages came there with enthusiasm to man their first hawks.

With the other falconers, Dickon learned to give absolute obedience to Adam. A boy might come from the noblest house in the land, but he would still be dismissed from the hawk houses if he had not washed his hands before handling his hawk or had ignored some minor rule. A squire approaching knighthood, already handling his horse like a man, stood abashed before Master Adam, no matter who looked on, if he had flown his bird too often or too hard, however successfully.

Abashed too were those fastidious squires who liked to use musk or some other perfume, for peregrines hated strong, pungent scents and Master Adam's nose was even sharper than theirs.

The routine of the mews delighted Dickon. He loved to come early in the morning upon the rousing birds, to feed and bathe them, and to watch them weathering in their embroidered hoods, like a conclave of bishops, upon their perches in the sun.

Master Adam learned Dickon could be relied on to weigh food for each hawk with great exactness and to keep it perfectly clean, also to administer regularly the little stones that are given to hawks to aid their digestion. Before long he could tell at a glance which hawk was in fine fettle and which needed a change of diet.

The work of the mews was endless. New birds were brought in, eyases and passage hawks caught during their migration, wild with a season's hunting for their own food. These birds were keen and clever, capable of becoming the finest game hawks of all if successfully trained. When Dickon came to the castle, these birds were in full process of being manned, and occupied a great deal of Adam's time. The squires manned their own eyases.

Dickon noticed how some of the smaller birds, taken too early from the nest, continued to scream ceaselessly throughout their training, as if the habit of calling their parents would never be shed. Two of these became such a nuisance in the hawk house that in exasperation Master Adam turned them free. "Birds like these, taken too young from the nest, will continue to scream until old age stops their beaks," he said when Dickon wondered, for the birds were very handsome.

"Will they die, Master Adam?" he asked.

"No, they'll not die!" said the falconer ironically. "Not unless they cut their throats with their own screaming."

When, in November, the falconers arrived from Valkenswaard, in Holland, from Scotland, and from Wales, Dickon stood at Master Adam's elbow in the Great Hall to see new hawks chosen.

The Earl chose a fine Flemish bird, whose wings were long, but fine and strong. He might become a high flier, and a swift one too. A falcon from Scotland was selected, but its mate was rejected for a fault in one of her wings.

"Do you see here?" Master Adam called to Dickon, and bade him run his finger down the outstretched wing. The faintest ridge across the spread feathers betrayed a weakness that might break in flight. At some time during her early life the eyas had been starved, and the hunger trace would remain till new feathers replaced the old.

A shy bird from Wales was chosen. The Welsh falconer who brought the bird, perched upon a cadge, or frame, that hung round his neck, conversed with the master falconer when the business was over.

"There is an eyrie that I know of at the place of St. David's!" he said. "Very fine birds are to be found there in the spring. You must bring that boy with you and we will send him down the cliff to fetch them up! My lord will never fly better falcons than are bred on the cliffs of Wales!"

As Dickon developed in skill, all the castle boys

treated him with respect. Here before them was
that rare thing Master Adam spoke of so fre-
quently but could never seem to find among their
ranks—a born falconer, one who in a few short
months could hood and unhood the shyest bird
without a fuss. They began to go to Dickon when
Master Adam was not available, partly for his
good nature and partly for his common sense and
skill.

The Earl's falconer never praised Dickon, but
seldom rated him. Days of high delight were those
when the old man allowed him to go hawking with
the squires, to carry the cadge for many a weary
mile over moor and fen. Then he would see, perhaps, the first hawk ringing her way up into the
pale sky of the winter's morning and would watch
the deadly tournament once the game was flushed.

When the sport was over, Dickon enjoyed re-
hooding the noble hawks, who so recently had
winged the heights of heaven. It rejoiced his heart
to have them so content and docile in his hands.
They might have chosen the wide wildness of
escape but had not.

Once home, the mews and outer courtyard became active with boys cooling their hawks in the
pale winter sunlight, exchanging comments on
the morning's sport as they walked to and fro.

For Dickon there were hawk houses to clean

and hawks' harness to mend. Sometimes there was a bruised feather to be mended by Adam. He often commanded Dickon to hold the hooded bird, as with firm but gentle fingers he spread the wing and dipped the injured feather into a jar filled with warm water. He showed Dickon how to pinch the spine of the feather above and below the bruise until it was quite soft, and then to smooth it gently upwards, following the line of the feathers until the hurt tissue appeared to be smoothed away.

Sometimes the eager owner stood beside Master Adam, and then it was he who was instructed, and even made to plunge his hand into the jar to carry out the treatment. But Adam found the birds struggled less in Dickon's hands, so without comment he often called the boy when such an operation was necessary.

The weeks came and went, boys grew and burst out of their liveries, needing new clothes; their piping voices broke and deepened. Yesterday's little page was today's lanky squire.

"The Welsh bird is promising well," Master Adam remarked to the Earl one day.

"Ay. I would like another from her eyrie," the Earl agreed. "But the Welsh squire, Gareth. What do you think of him? With that sullen humor, will

he ever make a game hawk, or is he likely to remain a goshawk to the end of his days and bring
no glory to us?"

"I do not know," Adam replied. "There is a
spirit behind him that is noble and chivalrous, but
he quarrels and stirs up his companions so fre-
quently that the best among them call him the
Crab."

The Earl laughed sardonically. "He is well
named!"

Gareth knew of the nickname, which infuriated
him. To crab was a hawking term used for a hawk
who, flown with a companion, attacked that mate
instead of stooping on the quarry. If it made a
habit of this, the bird was never allowed free near
its companions. The implications were clear
enough. Gareth seemed unable to live at peace
with others.

CHAPTER 12

At the Eyrie

SPRING ARRIVED, AND THE NEW HAWKS WERE flown at the wily rooks, giving great satisfaction.

Dickon, who had helped to man them, thrilled to see the skill with which the Scottish falcon, after flying once or twice with a trained hawk, set his own course and hunted down his rook with speed and energy. The Welsh bird, too, stooped like a bullet on the strongest rook that flew, avoiding the deadly beak and claws, to seize her prey by the head and tumble it to earth.

There had been losses among the hawks during the winter. Visitors bringing falcons had introduced a malady of the crop that played havoc with the peregrines. Gareth's bird had died, though he and Master Adam sat up all night with her, dosing her with an extraction of daisy leaves and herbs, and applying poultices to her swollen body.

Dickon went home at times, glad to find young Jack manfully flying his hawk. Dickon found Meg cumbrous and slow after the darting peregrines. He was fond of his home, but the life there held no attraction for him. His elder brother and his father laughed at him for the new manners he had learned from the squires. His mother, secretly proud of him, was embarrassed as with a being from another world. Young Jack, for all his pride of ownership, was chiefly concerned in what the goshawk could catch for the pot. Dickon was always glad when it was time to go back to the castle.

The Earl treated him now more as a falconer page than as a common assistant falconer. He had constant duties in the Great Hall, particularly at the high table, and the rumor went around among the pages that the Earl intended one day to make him a squire. This caused a certain ill feeling, not among the other squires and pages, but among the servants and underfalconers; only fear of Master

Adam prevented them from making Dickon's life a burden.

The Earl, whose eye was as far seeing as that of his favorite falcon, noticed the resentment, and took advantage of the needs of the mews to send Dickon away from the castle for a while. There would be falcons' eyries in the Pembrokeshire cliffs and, in company with Master Adam, Dickon was to ride down to the coast of Wales to capture some eyases.

Impulsively Gareth sought out Master Adam and begged to go too.

"What, and sleep in the open air, or under a rude shelter on the ground?" Master Adam scoffed, fixing the boy with his piercing blue eyes. "And swarm down cliffs overhanging the sea, with screaming falcons dashing at you from above and the sucking waves below?"

Gareth was silent. It was true his only thought had been to see his beloved Welsh coast again. He turned on his heel, biting his lip at the falconer's irony. But in the morning he asked the falconer again. This time Master Adam simply said that he must get permission from the Earl. This permission was granted, and the party clattered out over the drawbridge one morning in early summer.

With bundles strapped to their saddles, cadges on the cruppers, and falconers' bags about their waists, Dickon and Gareth felt properly equipped for their venture and proud of the unmistakable hallmarks of their trade.

At the Severn River a flat-bottomed boat carried their small company across, while the horses, stripped of saddles and cadges, swam behind. The ferryman related how a wild peregrine had pursued a woodcock across the river and, turning suddenly back, had dodged right across the bow of his boat. The peregrine had dived upon it, striking it with such force that she dashed her head against the bow and fell into the river. The boatman fished both bodies out of the water and laid them on the deck for dead. The woodcock recovered first and sped away across the river. The hawk, apparently lifeless, lay until the sun had dried her feathers, when all of a sudden she made off in the direction from which she had come and was seen no more.

"And if I had had a falconer's glove I'd have caught and sold her," the boatman said. "But I never had a rag beside me and my coat was too good to tear with such devil's claws as she had."

They climbed between a range of domelike hills, very beautiful and wooded, looking back upon the lands of home spread like a far carpet at their feet. Then for a long while the way wound through woods, and under the trees where the earth was bare a soil of a marvelous rose red took the place of their brown fields. But soon the red soil was swallowed up by black mountainside, precipice, and crag.

Dickon felt cramped and oppressed after the width of his Worcestershire plains. They met few people, even at the border hostelry where they spent the night. For the first time in months he was without a hawk to care for and this added to his depression. "I think I do not care for traveling," he told himself, feeling disconsolate.

As they rode beyond the border country, men dwelt in their castles much as they dwelt in England, feeling secure and welcoming guests or strangers. So Dickon met landlords and nobles, fellow travelers and natives, as varied as ever came to Castle Alden. He lodged in fine places or in stark ones, with merry hosts and somber, all the way across the land of Wales.

The coast, which for days, according to Master Adam, had been close on their left hand, never could be seen, because of the rough ground and rolling hills that screened it from sight. At last they struggled down a rough track to a stony bay with black cliffs, where islands stood off to sea, thrashed by the milk-white frenzy of waters. When they had crossed a marshy valley and climbed again, they came to the place made holy seven hundred years ago or more by St. David.

From there a northward road led them over moors to a high headland overlooking the sea, where the setting sun gilded the small hovel of Morgan, the Welsh falconer.

Some time before dark they walked out to the headland, where for the first time Dickon realized the power of this mighty force, the ocean, raging at his feet two hundred feet below the black cliffs. He leaned over, to gauge the void beneath him, and witnessed the sucking wash of waves receding from caves that were never dry. The feeling that enveloped him was colder and more dreadful than fear. He stared, appalled, at Gareth, who leaped lightly and fearlessly among the rocks as if he enjoyed the scene below.

Dickon shut his eyes as small, stout puffins hurtled off the cliff toward the sea, skimming the surface with the busy ease of long familiarity. A stone, dislodged, fell noiseless into the abyss, just as he might fall himself, thought Dickon, just as he would fall if he did not close his eyes and scramble back to the reassurance of firm turf and clumps of thyme.

Old Morgan pointed north, where the cliffs rose even higher. The peregrines' eyrie was there, he

said, and being mid-June it was high time the
eyases were taken, for they were nearly plumed
and would soon leave the nest. Another week,
Morgan said, and Master Adam would have lost
them.

This eyrie, the old man told them, was historic.
The peregrines that nested there bred from the
same strain century after century. King Athelstan
of England had taken his falcons from it before
the Conqueror came, and tales about it occupied
the first long hours of the night, when Dickon
swung in imagination over the awful precipice and
woke with fearful spasms, dreaming that he was
falling.

"Stay quiet!" Gareth ordered, heedless that he
himself tossed and turned continuously. He was
outraged at having to share a pallet with Dickon.

Suddenly the dawn came, and Dickon realized
the cottage had been silent for a long while. The
two falconers and Gareth were deeply asleep.
For a while he lay listening to the unaccustomed
roar of the sea far off at the foot of the cliffs, but
his mind was quiet now, as if so many hours of
terror had exhausted fear. Presently he crept from
his pallet and went outside. The beauty of early
morning in such a strange place bewildered him.
Beyond the sloping headland, the gray ocean
melted into a paler horizon that seemed more a

beginning than an end, for the sea went on and on westward, farther than imagination could follow. It was flecked now by hundreds of white flying gulls and whiter gleaming gannets.

The sea swept backward, almost encircling him, as if it would eventually cut off this rocky headland, making escape impossible save by the terrible cliffs.

Dickon turned his back on the sea, striking out in the only direction where he would not have to look at it—northeast across marshland, with a far view of quiet, rolling mountains flecked with gold. He ran downhill, glad to shed the sound of plunging water, his lungs thankful for draughts of fresh air after the stuffiness of the hut.

The hobbled horses whinnied to him. Then all was quiet, very quiet, and the wet marsh seeped through his shoes with the familiar coolness of marshes at home.

He looked for a heron. What a fine wild place to fly a falcon! There was no heron, but suddenly across the high clear sky appeared a falcon, sailing in from the sea. Before Dickon's eyes it circled higher, higher, as high as any hawk he had ever seen. Then like a shaft of light it stooped and struck, in the same moment, it seemed, that a snipe darted up the marsh toward Dickon. The peregrine killed within a stone's throw of him, darting up with the quarry in its claws almost into Dickon's face. He had a glimpse of the dark fierce eyes as the bird flashed by. Then it was gone over the headland.

The air seemed stiller than ever when it was gone, though there had been no sound. The silence of the hill stunned Dickon, who had never seen a wild hawk before, nor watched a stoop without hearing the shimmering song of little bells.

He raced breathlessly up the hill to view the end, which came even more dramatically than he had expected. The peregrine's mate flew up to meet him from the cliff. For a moment they trembled and sparred playfully at each other, and then she took the quarry from him in mid-air, diving down toward the nest, while he planed quickly away in search of more provisions.

The noble line of his wings was unmistakable— from tip to tip no semblance of a curve to mar his speed. That such a prize should be so free! thought Dickon. He would face a thousand precipices to capture the offspring of such a bird.

It was evening when they tramped to the cliffs. There were a pair of eyases, Morgan thought, but he had only seen them from his little boat at sea. The boys' eyes widened when they saw the bundles the old man brought from the dark depths of his house, the ropes and battered basket that had equipped a score of descents.

"I would not ride a kitten in that basket!" Gareth whispered to Dickon ruefully, but he was not really afraid, Dickon thought, or he would not joke so freely. His own heart throbbed with apprehension and his knees trembled, but rather than betray himself to Master Adam and the Welshman he shouldered the ropes and strode ahead.

They followed the cliffs for some distance while the sun slowly sank toward the west. There were two or three hours of daylight left, but there was night in the gulls' cries, and even the waves beat more softly.

Soon old Morgan stopped at a point on the cliff where the drop below was sheer to the sea. "This is the place!" he said. There was no sign of the parent birds.

The old Welshman explained that the young were fed every three hours, and as nothing could be heard of them they must lately have had a meal. He had watched their habits and knew the best time to make a capture.

"But if the birds return and come at you," he instructed the boys, "do not look at them, for they will do you no harm. And if they scream at you, stop your ears and do not listen."

The boys had not been told which of them was

to make the descent in the rough basket. All the instructions had been given to both, and they did not even know whether one or more descents would be made that evening. Master Adam looked at them and raised his eyebrows questioningly. Gareth stepped forward at once, ready to take his place in the frail basket old Morgan was preparing to lower from a spike driven between the rocks. He would have been insulted beyond endurance had Dickon taken the lead in this adventure, for he regarded every rock and chasm here on the Welsh coast as his own heritage.

Dickon could not avoid being struck by the change in Gareth's face as it disappeared below the cliff. He wore an expression of serenity and purpose and showed no sign of fear. Dickon wondered at his courage.

Master Adam, on one knee, was giving final instructions for the taking of the eyases, which were to be placed in the bottom of the basket wrapped in cloths. The moment he arrived on the eyrie ledge, Gareth was to tug on the rope to signify how many birds there were. Once the birds were in the basket and he wished to be pulled up, three tugs on the rope would give the signal.

It was a straight though steep descent, of no particular difficulty. Old Morgan knew just which spot would lower the basket most directly to the eyrie, but the overhang was such that Gareth dropped almost immediately out of sight. Dickon felt his stomach turn over as he lay peering over the void with his companions. He forgot that Gareth had played among crags on precipitous mountains since his birth and had more concern for the spiteful talons of his prey than for the rocks so far beneath him.

"Ha!" exclaimed Morgan, as the rope vibrated. "One, look you! One eyas only!"

A smaller tug followed the first.

"What is it? Half a tug? Half a bird is it?" asked the Welshman, curious.

One and a half tugs came unmistakably.

"An older and a younger eyas!" said Master Adam. "I hope he has the sense to leave the small one in the nest. It will scream till Michaelmas year and longer if we take it. Give the rope a pull, Master Morgan, and maybe he'll read it right!"

The Welsh falconer leaned so far beyond the edge of the precipice that Dickon turned away so as not to see him fall. Morgan screamed as he did so, "Take one, my lord! Take one!" But the high, thin voice was lost in the surge of water, in the cry of a thousand sea birds disturbed by the eyrie thief, in the wind blowing lightly across the abyss and tossing all sounds like playthings into the bowl of the air.

"He'll not be long with a single bird!" said Morgan. "His hands are well gloved and he will not need to leave the basket to take one only. There is no danger if a man stays in the basket, look you! But if he has to leave the basket and stand upon the ledge, then it is dangerous indeed. The ledge slopes downward to the sea except where the nest is, and a man has not a very good balance when he holds the rope in one hand and takes an eyas in the other. But if he stands in the basket then he is quite safe."

The old man rambled on while the minutes seemed like hours to Dickon. He forgot his giddiness in fixing his eyes on the rope, watching for the vibration that meant the signal to haul. Gratefully he thanked the saints that he was not down there standing upon the ledge, which was dangerous indeed.

"He is taking his time!" the Welshman complained after a while.

Master Adam said nothing.

Presently Morgan gave the rope a slight pull. Then with an exclamation he pulled again. "He is not in the basket!" he cried. "The boy has let it go. Feel there!"

Master Adam took the rope. Truth to tell, the rope came easily toward him and ran back slowly, checking as the basket bumped on the eyrie ledge. At the same time, far below them, they heard a cry that was not the call of a bird, but unmistakably the cry of Gareth.

"There is one place where maybe I can see him!" the Welshman said, thrusting the rope into Adam's hand. "Try this every two or three minutes while I go to see."

To their amazement they saw him scramble down the precipitous cliff at a point not twenty yards from them, and peer outward and downward. Then he waved his arms in the wildest excitement, and in a few moments was beside them again. "God save us! The lad is safe!" he cried. "He is on the ledge below the eyrie, and cannot return to it! We must send down more rope and lower the basket!" But although he paid out several yards of slack, there was no answering pull from the basket on the eyrie ledge. The rope dangled limply from their hands.

"It is fast on the shelf! Perhaps it has landed in the nest itself!" said Morgan. "We must shake the basket free."

"But what if there is an eyas in it?" Master Adam interrupted. "Could you see the birds just now?"

"No, I could see nothing of them. I could not

see the eyrie from there at all," said Morgan. "I could only see the legs of my lord Gareth standing on the ledge. He could not see me, either."

Another shout rose above the cry of the gulls.

"The boy is impatient!" said the Welsh falconer. "He will come to no harm where he is if he stands still. It is a better ledge than that other one!"

"Bring up the basket and I will go down to him," said Master Adam.

Morgan began to haul, and the basket came up with a struggling bundle in the bottom of it that revealed a fine young tiercel nearly ready to fly. Old Morgan bundled this bird into a bag and tested the rope and the basket.

"Look you, Master Adam," he said. "We are heavy men, you and I, and the basket must go twice down and twice up again. There is an overhang below that chafes the rope. This boy here is light. We will send him down."

"Yes, Master Adam, let me go down!" said Dickon automatically, but he felt the blood leave his face as he spoke.

The master falconer looked at him so long and searchingly that he quailed, afraid that his cowardice was known. His knees began to tremble again and thunder drummed in his ears, so that he only half heard Master Adam murmur some

words about his unwillingness to imperil Dickon's
life.

But perhaps it was of Gareth that they spoke,
for Morgan made fast a new length of rope and
Master Adam held the basket just over the cliff's
edge, for Dickon to step inside.

"Why should the boy have got himself into
such a place?" the Welsh falconer was babbling.
"It is easy to climb down there from the shelf
above. I did that once when I was young and had
dropped an eyas of value on the ledge. My father
left me there all night to teach me a lesson, for it
is not possible to get back alone. It was moonlight
that night and the falcons never ceased to scream
and dive at me. I nearly lost my wits, but it was
a beautiful eyas!"

"I'd leave my lord Gareth there to cool himself
if I had my way!" the English falconer said grimly.
"But we have the eyas safe."

Then their voices faded above him as Dickon
swung slowly down the abyss. A hundred feet
below, Morgan had said, was the eyrie. He could
not bear to open his eyes to look for Gareth, but
he could not close them either, because he must
keep the basket from chafing against the rocks.
When the overhang was passed, he swung dizzily
for a moment, spinning round and round, before
he dared reach out a hand to steady himself

against the cliff face. Down, down—he was getting used to the sensation. So long as he did not look below, things were better.

Suddenly, far beneath him, he heard a shout. Gareth had seen him coming and was hailing him, but even now he dared not look. He knew that the two of them could not ascend together. Neither the rope nor the basket was strong enough. Old Morgan had told him to stand on the shelf when he reached the eyrie, and to lower the basket to Gareth, who would then be pulled up to him.

"And let him wait there," Morgan added, "while you come to the top."

Another shout came from Gareth, this time a greeting and much closer. Then there was a jolt and a fearsome shriek as the basket bumped to a standstill on the eyrie ledge, almost on the head of a small, fluffy eyas who sat in a tangle of twigs, bones, and torn feathers, spitting with rage and indignation at this second violation of her nursery.

"Ho, Dickon!" cried Gareth impatiently, and at last Dickon had to look down, grasping the edge of the basket to give him courage.

Gareth was, in fact, only a few feet below the eyrie ledge, on a small, level shelf that hung between the cliff and certain death below. On this ledge he perched helpless, just too far from the eyrie to spring back. He was obviously in pain from one ankle, which he spared as well as he could by standing on one leg. Dickon gasped to see him balanced there. Surely at any moment he would topple into the sea beneath.

"Lower the basket, man!" Gareth pleaded, with more penitence than fear. "The gulls are born to stand on one leg from Easter till Candlemas, but not I! Lower the basket!"

Dickon scrambled out, giving a double tug to the rope, which meant the next stage had begun.

The eyas, exhausted for the moment with battering and pecking at the basket, fell silent while he bestrode her nest. His back to the cliff, Dickon saw the basket lowered to Gareth below. Then the rope vibrated to a double tug, and soon Gareth's face was looking up at him. Again the basket landed on the ledge, and the screaming eyas shuffled aside to avoid being crushed between the two of them.

"By the saints!" exclaimed Gareth. "I would not spend another hour on that pin rack by my own choice!"

"How did you get there?" asked Dickon.

"Why—I *went* by my own choice!" laughed Gareth, who seemed to view the whole adventure as a joke. "The tiercel clawed at me so he caused my gauntlet to fall out of my belt onto the ledge. I only paused to put the hawk in the basket before going below to fetch it. But there is a trick in it," the squire continued, "for the way back from that ledge is all but impossible, and my ankle is hurt so I cannot use it. Look down, Dickon!" he added excitedly. "Do you see? If the gauntlet had not fallen on the ledge it must have dropped two hundred feet into that swirling pool and been sucked into the caves below!"

Dickon shuddered but would not look.

"Ah, well," said Gareth, "I'll get up aloft and face Master Adam's wrath! But I took a pretty eyas for him. Did you see him for yourself?"

"Yes, it was a fine bird!" Dickon agreed faintly. Above all he wished to get into the basket and leave this horrible place. "Master Adam said you were to cool your spirits on this ledge till the basket returned for you," he said weakly.

"Now, good Dickon, you heard him wrong!" Gareth pleaded, laughing. "There is not a level square inch here where I can rest my broken foot. I will not stand another hour like a sea gull for Master Adam's pleasure. Wait for me, good Dickon, while I get to the top and send down the basket. This is a poor spot to change places— scarcely room for two men to stand, and we may even kick the poor eyas into the sea. What a small thing it is! The tiercel must be the elder by some weeks."

As he spoke he pulled the rope and, still chatting carelessly, began his journey up the rock face, as cool as if he had set out for a morning's ride or to break a lance in friendly combat with a friend.

Oh, for such coolness! Dickon thought. He dared not even turn his back to the abyss and face the rock. Now he must close his eyes. But when he closed them he felt his body sway, while the world turned round about him. The little eyas on the edge of the nest began a new and anguished screaming, and began to flap and struggle so that he feared she would fall off the ledge.

Grimly focusing on the food fragments at his feet, Dickon pushed the wing of a dead pigeon toward her, but the eyas attacked him like a fury, sinking beak and claw into his ankle, and tearing his soft buckskin shoes. The pain was sharp and unexpected and he could not protect himself. His hands were bare and his only defense was to kick the bird off the ledge. This he would not do, and if he had, the movement might have jerked him after her. So he froze into immobility while the spitting creature tore at his stocking and uttered shrill wailing cries.

Suddenly a new danger threatened Dickon from the air. After hunting for their hungry young far to the north, the peregrines had returned. Whether they had sensed the danger to their family from a distance, or whether from the heights they ruled they saw the marauders gathered on the cliff top, no one could say. But as Dickon raised his eyes to the sky to avoid the danger everywhere surrounding him, he saw the winged avengers diving on him, and his blood turned cold.

He was utterly exposed and could not move hand or foot to save himself. His fingers clung desperately to the chinks in the rock at his back. His feet and calves were braced against the shelf. The slightest movement of his legs would bring a new assault from the needle beak and the claws of the eyas, who, seeing her parents, began to scream again most piteously.

In the long, terrifying moment when he saw the birds coming, Dickon had the wild inclination to fling himself over the edge into the sea. Anything rather than lose his eyes to those murderous claws!

Then the memory of another vigil came back to him forcefully. He had been in deadly danger in a beech tree, facing death, and again on account of a hawk. At the time that danger had seemed more terrible than anything he had imagined; it was associated with the same dizziness and sweating fear. And he had escaped!

The falcons would not touch him. Old Morgan had said he was to ignore them! Ignore two steel arrows approaching him at a hundred miles an hour, growing larger, louder, larger, till darkness shut out the light? A rush of air swept past him, then another, and he flung up both hands to shield his eyes.

The falcons were below him, the steely blue of the tiercel's back rolling lightly from side to side as he crossed the chasm and darted up above the sea. While he still watched, the female dived on him. He saw the small feathers stand out below her bill, the purpose expressed in her dark bright eye. She passed within an arm's length of him, screaming, but the tiercel with even fiercer cries brushed his cap. The eyas shrieked its helplessness, goading the parents, who stooped from closer and closer range, the air in a turmoil from their wingbeats.

Dickon stood rigid, one arm across his eyes, expecting to have his fingers ripped or his head slashed open. He could not number the attacks nor take any account of the time that had passed since Gareth mounted the cliff. When suddenly something knocked his head, he thought, Now they have me! He might have ducked and fallen had not the basket landed beside him, giving the unfortunate eyas yet another buffet that set all three birds screaming till the echoes rang.

Dickon thought afterwards that he jumped into the basket before it fairly landed in the nest.

No journey to heaven could be so welcome as that ascent of the cliff, though in one last frenzied attack the talon of one of the falcons drew blood from Dickon's ear. But his heart was so thankful that it was almost with Gareth's nonchalance that he stepped onto the turf at the top of the cliff and looked into Adam's anxious face.

The old falconer seemed as moved as Dickon had ever seen him. He even put an arm round the boy's shoulders and examined his torn ear.

"I never saw it happen before!" said the old Welshman. "I have seen them attack. Yes, but I never saw them touch a man. It is a wonder the boy was not dashed to his death below!"

"It was as ugly a place as ever I dreamed of!" Gareth agreed, nursing his injured foot on the grass and chewing a piece of thyme.

The old Welshman trotted down the hill to bring up his pony for the wounded squire, while Master Adam picked up the sack and slowly followed him.

A week later they took the younger bird. This time Dickon was lowered down the cliff to the eyrie with hardly a qualm. Gareth, because of his former foolishness, was not given the chance to descend, but he showed no resentment.

Presently they left the Welsh coast to ride back to England.

CHAPTER 13

Knighthood

WHEN THEY RETURNED TO CASTLE ALDEN, THEY found Edward of Lentwardine about to be made a knight.

The long years of education in chivalry had passed, and boyhood, even youth, was over for Lentwardine. Old for his years, he walked gravely among the scenes set in his honor, the preparations for tournament, for banqueting, and the housing of many guests.

As his knighthood approached, Edward seemed to recede farther and farther from the bustle of castle life. It was not that he set himself above his companions, for no one ever failed to draw a kindly word from him or a note of sympathy when needed, but in spirit he far surpassed the rest. His counsel and conversation were sought by the many friends and acquaintances of the Earl who were visiting at the castle, and who hunted and hawked and jousted. Because his life was soon to lead him into savage places, he needs must put aside the lure and gauntlet on many a merry occasion, in order to devote himself to all manner of practice for battle—swordsmanship and tilting, attack and defense. He rode with hardened warriors mile after weary mile in full armor, only to fight a sally in the tiltyard on his return, all to harden his muscles and better his endurance for the tasks and trials to come.

Because he was to ride against the faithless, Lentwardine spent long hours in the chapel contemplating the Crusade he had chosen—not as many choose it, in the cause of valor and glory, but because he was to do battle for his deepest love of God.

The returning travelers found the courtyard in a hubbub, the halls filled with strangers, many wearing the livery of Lentwardine's house. For his father had come to witness his knighting, and those who saw the tall baron with the calm, contemplative face knew from whence came Edward's chivalry.

The next morning the Earl came to the mews to praise the eyases. He agreed with Master Adam that the big tiercel was the finer bird. The falcon seemed nervous and puny, as if the shock of the first kidnapping had left its mark. She was put out to hack, to recover from the long journey, while Dickon was told he could begin to man the stronger tiercel.

Proud beyond measure, he was crossing the courtyard with his head held high when he came face to face with Lentwardine, who had just made his farewells as a squire to his old friend and tutor Master Adam. Now he was about to join his squires of honor for a visit to the barber, who would shave his head in the fashion ordered by the coming ceremony.

Lentwardine was smiling, as if a joke shared with the old falconer still hung about him. He clapped a friendly hand on Dickon's shoulder. "I hear we both keep a vigil tonight, friend!" he exclaimed. "One day you shall ride behind me, Dick Falconer! Say a prayer for me tonight!"

The astonished boy stammered some reply before Edward disappeared. The young man had as good as called him a fellow squire, he who was born in a cottage and might not wear the clothes of a gentleman. But he had asked him to ride behind him, as a squire might do, and had given him a surname besides.

Lentwardine and his two squires of honor went through the solemn ritual preceding knighthood, first a bath in a room hung with rich tapestries and fair linen. His father and the Earl of Alden joined him there to instruct and question him in the laws of chivalry. The Earl then poured water from the bath on Edward's head, signing his left shoulder with the sign of the cross.

Having undergone this ceremony of purification, the young knight-to-be was led by the squires to a bed unadorned by coverlets or costly hangings. There he would rest in the symbolism of the peace that is found in Paradise by the pure in heart.

Now they put on him a plain white shirt to prove him clean from all previous sin. Over this they threw a red robe the color of the blood he would readily shed in the service of his God; and as if to remind him that blood may not be lightly spilled, a long black garment topped the rest, the symbol of mortality.

Gravely the two older knights returned to lead him to the chapel. With his father on Edward's right hand and the Earl on his left they paced the breadth of the castle yard, preceded by the two squires, joined outside the ceremonial chambers by minstrels and musicians. The whole castle company were gathered in solemnity to watch the young knight walking to his vigil, remaining outside as he passed out of sight into the shadows of the chapel.

The priest, Father Bartholomew, and a candle bearer entered the chapel and remained there, but before long the two older men reappeared, returning to their own quarters in the castle. Each had saluted the young man with a kiss on the cheek before they retired, leaving him to long deep hours of prayer, kneeling before the altar, where already his armor lay piled beside his sword, lance, and helmet.

In the small chamber behind the chapel Dickon walked and watched with the new falcon from which so much was expected, following in his mind's eye the ceremony that had been related to him by the pages—penetrating the thick walls in imagination to see the squire kneeling beside his armor, vowing his vows to dedicate his life to obedience to the will of God.

Dickon, calming and cherishing and coaxing the proud spirit of the bird in his hand, marveled that a man might grow so noble as Lentwardine. He despised himself and his hopes, so presumptuous and unfounded. No one would make a squire of an oaf like himself; and if he might stay with his hawks what more could he desire? To fly them, of course, came the immediate answer, as if spoken aloud in the darkness.

Dickon turned his attention to his bird. All the chivalry and grace, the charm and patience he had learned in the castle hall, went into his handling of this beloved hawk. Though he himself had captured the falcon, he loved the tiercel best. He thought he recognized, too, the splendid carriage of the father bird who had stooped to kill the snipe in the marshes.

Toward dawn Dickon listened for a sound from the chapel, but the thick walls kept their counsel. He knew, because the squires had told him, that Lentwardine would confess to a priest, hear mass, and make his Communion.

Awed by the silence, Dickon was grateful for the companionship of the hawk. The night had drawn them close; there had been no battle of wills between them from the first. At last he heard the far-off door of the chapel close with a clang.

The vigil ended and his Communion made, the young knight had lit a candle to the glory of God and was gone out into the morning to break his long fast and rest before the concluding part of the ceremony.

Dickon saw nothing of the ceremony that followed during the day, but he watched from afar the thronging crowds that lined the walls when Edward went, with friends, to dedicate his sword to the service of God, the Church, the poor, and the oppressed.

Master Adam told him later about the ceremony. The old falconer described the crowd in the Great Hall and the Earl on his dais, waiting to receive the young man, who walked the length of the Hall to kneel before him and declare his desire to be a good and faithful knight to the end of his days. Now he stood up to don the gilded spurs. One was put on by his father and the second by another knight of high repute, each making the sign of the cross on the young man's knee.

His friends then armed him with all his armor, ending with the sword which the Earl himself buckled round his waist. Then he knelt before the Earl, who struck him smartly on the shoulder and cried, "Rise, Sir Edward! Be thou a good knight!"

The ceremony finished, the entire household repaired to the field of tournament where the new knight was to show his worth, and tilt with many an opponent in front of the Earl, his own father, and the assembled company.

CHAPTER 14

The Hawk Fair

To complete his team for the winter hawking the Earl decided to send his head falconer with Dickon to Valkenswaard in Holland, to the great hawk fair held every autumn. To make two great journeys in so short a space of time left Dickon breathless.

He went to bid Edward of Lentwardine good-by, for when they returned from Holland Lentwardine would be off to the Crusades.

"When I return I'll make thee my own squire, if the Earl allows. We'll fly the hawks at the heron together on the Alden marshes!" Lentwardine cried, clapping Dickon on the shoulder.

Early in the morning Dickon and Master Adam made their Communion in the chapel before riding away to the port of London, where they would board a ship for Holland.

The crossing of the English Channel was as hard as Dickon had ever expected it to be. The voyage seemed to go on for hours, with the ship wallowing, plunging and rolling, while the very thought of food was sickening. They reached harbor at last, and it was a foreign world with a clack of foreign tongues, a smell of foreign drains and foods and cooking, a world where only their own horses and the harness on their backs still smelled English. It was a world too where the earth still heaved and swung and rolled long after Dickon sat in the saddle to follow Master Adam on the high road to Valkenswaard.

The little town of Valkenswaard in North Brabant saw the daily migration, in autumn, of hundreds of southward-traveling birds. Now it was preparing for the hawk fair to be held a fortnight later.

Adam and Dickon were to stay in the cottage of Pjieter, a falcon trapper whose family had netted hawks for generations past. Dickon soon learned to watch the sky. Within a day he realized that the bustle in the town was nothing to that which went on overhead. That high moving stain on a cloud was a formation of teal flying south. The short rush, low over the roofs, of a flock of linnets was a stage in their journey from the perilous cliffs of the north to the kindly south. The tired rows of swallows on the gables had traveled for hundreds of miles, but their journey was not yet done.

Master Adam watched with him, joined sometimes by old Pjieter, who explained that when such a flock, and such another, had ceased to pass overhead, the falcons would be coming. The old hawks would come first, Master Adam told Dickon, and later the red hawks, the hawks of the year, in their ruddy plumage, which changed after their first moulting. He was seeking a passage hawk for their team, for these often made splendid game hawks.

If Pjieter failed to catch a fine haggard for them, they would find one in the market afterward. After the migration was over, the choice of birds for sale would be infinite, only the prices might be very high.

Dickon walked out on the heath to see the small huts erected there by the falcon catchers, from which they trapped the hawks as they stooped to hunt on the heath in the early dawn. One morning he returned in a state of agitation. "I have seen a hawk on the plain!" he cried to Master Adam.

The falconer smiled at his excitement, for he knew some birds had already been captured. That evening old Pjieter and Master Adam left the house before dark, to spend the night in a turf hut on the plain, and try their luck in the morning.

Bitterly disappointed at being left behind, Dickon hardly touched the supper that Pjieter's wife set before him. A knocking came on the door. There followed a long conversation between Pjieter's wife and a man outside. Then a head poked into the room, accompanied by a hand with a beckoning finger. Dickon saw that the man carried a bag with pigeons in it, and with a sudden upsurging of his heart remembered that old Pjieter carried just such another. This man was Pjieter's brother, inviting him to go out on the heath.

He followed the man into the night, past small silent huts where men slept or watched, farther and farther into the hunting ground of the hawks. At last they crept into a hutch so cramped and small that it barely held even a man and a boy lying on their stomachs with their heads on their arms, to sleep the night away. But before they slept the man crept out with his bag of pigeons, returning empty-handed. Dickon heard the deep breathing of the falcon catcher fade into the rhythm of sleep and, being too cramped to move, suffered agonies before a kind of numbness let him doze.

The long night shed one layer of darkness and the sky paled in the east. Gradually each blade and bush on the heath became a silhouette against the sky, and Dickon saw a handful of birds on a perch not far from their hiding place. These moved and stretched and preened as the dawn broke. The hoarse notes they uttered in the growing light told him they were butcher birds. The falcon catcher was awake, too, watching them.

The pigeons were invisible, hidden perhaps in a smaller hut covered with turf to the right of the butcher birds' perch. Beyond this a pole pierced the sky, threaded by a thin cord that flapped a little in the breeze. Dickon saw his companion's fingers close on other cords trailing from him through the grass. He could not believe that such a primitive contraption would snare so wild and unpredictable a traveler as a falcon.

Suddenly the butcher birds began to shriek in such an agonized chorus that Dickon's pulses leapt. There was no mistaking the agitation in their cries, and what should cause such agitation but a hawk? Then a fully grown buck rabbit tore past them, with a wild goshawk half a second behind him.

Presently the birds cried again, and now it was a kite passing over. Then there was a long silence. Again the butcher birds protested. This time, for no reason that Dickon could guess, the catcher showed interest. Propelling himself very slightly forward on his elbows he took charge of the hidden cords and peeped outside. The birds were stirring again. Some new danger threatened in the brightening morning sky, and their excitement was shared by the chief watcher below.

The man's hands tightened on one of the cords, and from the smaller hut ahead a white pigeon was released. The cord, drawn through a hole on the top of the pole, pulled it toward the summit, where it flew round in the first rays of the sun, drawing all attention to itself.

Dickon never saw the splendid stoop of the wild haggard above, but the pigeon did, for it dived and the catcher slackened the cord. The hawk flew up over the hut as the captive bird reached safety. Dickon had a glimpse of the long blue wings tipped with black and felt the rush of air pass over his head.

But the drama was not over. The catcher knew

that the puzzled falcon was waiting above them, watching for the prey that had so narrowly escaped her talons. His fingers fumbled in the grass for a second string, and Dickon saw the other pigeon being drawn, fluttering, toward a netted arch covered with moss and pegged to the turf. This was the trap itself.

The capture ended in a movement so calculated and effortless that it only took a few seconds. The cord, passing around pegs, drew the pigeon behind the bow of the net. The falcon stooped like the flash of a blade, and as she landed, a swift twitch from a thinner cord dropped the second bow of the net over her head. It was over.

Breathing fast, Dickon followed the trapper to the trap. Pjieter's brother had donned thick gauntlets now. He picked up the unharmed pigeon and gave it to Dickon, then gently gathered the furious prisoner and eased her head first into a toeless stocking, uttering all kinds of endearing phrases and stroking her through the yarn.

She was a beautiful hawk, long of wing and tail, with splendid talons and a full, round restless eye. Dickon's heart thrilled toward her, but Pjieter's brother pointed to the butcher birds. Dickon had to detach and put them into a little cage, where some morsels of meat awaited them. Then he must put both pigeons in a bag and follow the falcon catcher home.

Master Adam and Pjieter were already at the house, drinking bowls of coffee and eating bread and cheese. They had captured a smaller falcon, which lacked a claw in one talon. Pjieter meant to sell her in the market. Master Adam said she was a very brave bird but of no use to himself. He opened his eyes at the blue falcon and became tense with interest, a sign Dickon had learned to recognize when he really admired a hawk. He bargained rapidly with the catcher, Pjieter translating.

Dickon guessed the brother thought he could get a better price in the coming market than the English falconer offered.

Master Adam fell very silent. Presently he had a long conversation with Pjieter, who arranged a new meeting in the town with his brother over a bottle of wine. The price of the hawk had gone up now. There was further argument and disagreement. Master Adam went into a dark hut to have another look at the bird, while Dickon waited outside in great agony of mind. But presently money passed, and the blue falcon became the property of Castle Alden.

Immediately Master Adam was in his most

genial humor, and the rest of their stay was as pleasant as could have been wished for. The master falconer knew he had paid a larger price than he had intended to, but the bird was worth the money, and he could begin its training at once. He had brought Dickon for that purpose, and the boy felt keen delight the first time he took upon his fist the falcon whose capture he had witnessed.

She was so dignified and, once hooded, so still, winning his heart by her patience and discretion. He hoped to make her education fine and swift. With Master Adam he shared the training of the first days, loving and taming her, and at last could carry her proudly in the town, a witness to his falconry.

Pjieter's brother took Dickon out again, and this time they brought in a red tiercel, and another time a pretty falcon, but the blue hawk stood high above them in quality. Master Adam bought a dark falcon at the market.

Winter blew a sudden chill into the autumn air, receding as rapidly, but leaving the legacy of shortening days, brief frosty sunsets, and skies empty of birds. Master Adam and Dickon made their farewells and rode back to the coast in company with many others of their kind.

The boat that took them back to England held

a large company of falconers, who found pleasure in exchanging tales of their experiences and showing off their hawks to one another. Among them was a boy younger than Dickon, called Simon, who showed great dexterity in handling a hawk, and the two drew close during the voyage, tending and feeding their birds together.

There was another falcon on board so closely resembling Dickon's that he pointed it out to Master Adam, but the owner proved strangely unfriendly, disappearing with his hawk to some dark corner under the pretext that it was nervous.

"Is yonder your master falconer?" Dickon asked Simon, when they put out on a calm sea the first morning and he saw the two conversing.

"Nay, I do not know him at all," the boy said shortly.

The voyage took three days in all, for they stayed at anchor many hours outside the port. The November sunshine was warm enough to sun the hawks upon the deck, and the small space was peopled by this hooded company watched by their jealous owners. Only the stranger's falcon stayed hidden in the hold, much pitied by the boys.

On the second evening the master falconers collected in the captain's quarters to drink wine with him, Master Adam among them, leaving Dickon in charge of the hawks. He had fed them in the cramped quarters allotted to him when Simon came hurriedly to his side.

"Here is a falconer with a sick hawk. Go and fetch your master. He will advise us. Pray fetch him and I will watch your hawk."

Dickon hesitated. "Tell the falconer Master Adam is in the captain's quarters. I know he will come," he said.

"Nay, my acquaintance cannot leave his bird," said the boy impatiently. "Go ask your master! I cannot leave my own bird. She bates and quakes and overheats tonight. But I will bring her here and watch the three hawks together."

He was so urgent and persuasive that Dickon went, speeding along the deck, weaving and dodging between the voyagers, who cuffed and buffeted him as their fancy took them. One put out a purposeful foot and sent him sprawling headlong, but it was not a time to show vexation. Picking himself up, Dickon ran on and pushed his way into the crowded cabin. There Dickon saw Master Adam in conversation with the sour-faced falconer who kept his bird so carefully apart.

The man saw Dickon, and deliberately set himself between the youth and his falconer, so that in the crowded space Master Adam could not see the boy. Dickon squared his elbows and shoved in vain. The man was made of iron. Finally, like a battering ram, making use of what small space there was, he lowered his head and butted the falconer in the ribs. The man let out a roar of pain and turned to strike the boy. At the same moment Dickon slipped under his arm and Master Adam saw him at last.

"Out of here! I cannot hear a word nor understand you!" he shouted above the din, pushing Dickon before him to the door. "Is all well with the hawks?" he demanded.

"Ours are well, but another man's is sick and they are asking your advice, Master Adam!" Dickon said, panting from the struggle.

"Why, good Master Adam, that is why *I* sought you out!" the other falconer, who had followed them, exclaimed with a sudden change of tone. "My bird has been taken with the craye. I have no remedy at sea. Tell me, pray, what sorcery or simples do you advise?"

He babbled on so ceaselessly that Dickon thought he had drunk too much wine, holding Master Adam affectionately by the sleeve and waxing eloquent over the probable fate of his poor bird if Master Adam would not give his valuable advice.

The master falconer tried to disengage himself from the babbler, who chattered ceaselessly, holding Master Adam firmly by the shoulder.

"Back to your hawks!" Master Adam said over his shoulder to Dickon.

Dickon went rapidly. He had stayed away too long. The tiny corner where the birds lived was deserted except for the falcons. Simon had not kept his promise to watch them while he was gone. The falling darkness barely outlined the two slender bodies, as they drowsed on their perches.

Roused by his return, the hawks began to settle down again for the night, and it was the pattern of their movements, the tiny habits and noises to which he had become accustomed during the last days and weeks, that told him instinctively a change had come over the birds.

Dickon knew every rustle and breath of the blue hawk he had trained. After days and nights spent in her company he felt he could count her feathers, even in the dark. And she was not moving as his falcon moved. There was even a hint of hoarseness in her breathing. It did not need Master Adam's lantern swung into the corner at last to tell Dickon that the falcon on the perch was not his own.

The master falconer stared, amazed at Dickon's tale, for by the lantern light the bird seemed identical. Passing a gentle hand under her train he raised the silver varvels. They bore the arms of Alden. The harness, the hood, were all the same.

Dickon was frantic. "You can see for yourself,

Master Adam! The bird is *not* ours!" he cried. "Let me find the boy Simon whom I left here and I will have the truth from him!"

Simon seemed dazed when Dickon dragged him from his own hawk to face Master Adam. "Why, I only left your hawks a moment ago!" he muttered. "No one came nor went while I was here! I left as I saw your lantern approach. I would not harm your bird, my friend!"

"I had no lantern!" Dickon cried. "It was Master Adam who came with the light."

"But what do you blame me for?" the boy asked. "No harm has come to your bird! I see no danger to her!"

"It is not our falcon! This is another bird!" Dickon insisted, frantic that Master Adam should shake his head and examine the hawk so doubtfully. "Say it is not our falcon, Master Adam!"

"Without doubt it is another bird!" the falconer replied gravely. Then he murmured, "But if any would agree who has not handled her, I would not like to say!"

"Not your bird, good master!" cried the boy, and now Dickon heard the note of falseness in the protest. "But, master, your bird is the talk of all the ship, and here she is. I never saw a finer!"

"Our bird is in good health, and stands a little

taller than this one. This falcon has a touch of the pantas or I am much mistaken," Master Adam mused. "And by daylight I'll vow there is less blue in her wings."

"Daylight will prove it!" agreed Simon with a feigned yawn.

Master Adam remarked, "I'll not wait till morning. There is another falcon on this boat that greatly resembles ours. Where is she kept?"

"It was her master that spoke to you, on the deck!" said Dickon eagerly. "Let me fetch him, good Master Adam, for there is a strange puzzle here, and we must have it out."

Master Adam went himself to fetch the falconer, while Simon slipped away, leaving Dickon burning with angry impatience beside his hawks. The falconer they sought was lying under the captain's table in a drunken stupor that nothing would rouse. But the other falconers, when they heard Master Adam's strange story, accompanied him to the mews and added their conjectures as to the identity of the falcon. They were much disappointed to find a falcon so similar in every point that one and all declared Master Adam must be mistaken. The captain's wine had gone to his head, they laughed, and his boy was an idiot!

Even in the lantern light Dickon saw his master's face turning a dark and ugly red at their jeering, for to suggest that a falconer did not know his own bird was insult indeed, and well the falconers knew it. They would not say outright the words at which they hinted.

"Find me the other bird and I'll prove it!" said Master Adam.

Simon had crept up to hear the argument.

"Where is the falcon we spoke of yesterday and today, the bird whose master hid her away?" Dickon asked him harshly. "*You* know which bird I speak of!"

"Ay-ay! But I do not know where she is kept! Ask her falconer!" said the boy, half defiant, half awkward.

"Her falconer is lying drunk. You told me you had seen her in the dark hold! Go and fetch her!" Dickon cried loudly.

"Ay! Fetch her, boy! We'll see for ourselves!" cried the company of falconers, sensing some sport.

"I dare not take another man's hawk!" the boy began, but a couple of men hurried him away, and their footsteps clattered down the narrow ladder to the hold.

Dickon and Master Adam gazed in relief and gratitude at the falcon that was brought into the

light, for to both of them there was no mistaking
their blue peregrine. The birds *had* been changed.

"Why, they are as alike as two breast feathers!"
the falconers exclaimed in wonder. "No blame to a
man for mistaking the two! Pardon, Master Falconer of Alden, but we would have done the same.
All is well. No one has taken your bird."

"But indeed they have!" Master Adam declared.
"That bird from the hold is mine. And I charge
this rascal that he exchanged the hawks tonight
while I was engaged by the bird's falconer. The
deceit was well planned ahead!"

"Good master, how can it be true?" the boy ex-
postulated. "I had three hawks to care for! I could
not steal yours and watch them at the same time,
and no one came or went all the time I was there!
No sir, you are mistaken. This *is* your hawk. Do
you not agree, good masters?"

There was a chorus of "Ay!" from the company,
and much laughter.

"I'll prove it, masters!" Dickon shouted. "It is
the habit of our bird to bob, most daintily, when
offered something of sweet taste. I never saw a
bird so full of courtesy. Let me show you!"

The lights were subdued till barely enough remained for the hawks, now unhooded, to see the
dainties offered them. Both, having been fed, hesi-

tated at first. Then the falcon on the perch took the titbit forcefully, while the other, who had come from the hold, made her pretty obeisance before gently taking the morsel in her bill.

A sound of surprise and admiration rose from the crowd. The gesture was so unusual that a murmur of anger against the boy Simon began to be heard. He tried to slip through the crowd, but every arm prevented him. While some held him prisoner, others went to rout out the falconer from under the captain's table, where they guessed his stupor was pretended. Sailors and captain hurried after. The ship was in an uproar.

Hastily Master Adam secured his own hawks where the noise would least disturb them, while a kindly falconer, having changed the harness, took the innocent impostor back to the hold.

But nothing could be proved against either boy or falconer. The falconer, all had to agree, had been in their company the whole while and feigned great astonishment at the whole business. The boy Simon now hastily announced he had not stayed with the Alden hawks all the while he had promised, but had left them almost immediately.

Since no one stood to gain a penny except these two, no other guilty person could be named, and the severe penalty of such a crime was avoided.

But to teach him a lesson, the captain had the ship hove to and flung the boy Simon overboard.

As he watched him struggle like a rat to the ship's side through the black waves Dickon forgave him, for he could hardly swim and must have been terrified.

CHAPTER 15

Battle

THE HOMECOMING THAT SHOULD HAVE BEEN SO
joyful was tinged with tragedy. They felt the
shadow of it even before they crossed the drawbridge, acknowledging a muted greeting from the
men-at-arms.

The castle was crowded with people, but the
tense atmosphere, the sparse welcome and lack of
interest which persisted till they reached their
own quarters, widened Dickon's eyes and oppressed him fearfully. Master Adam spurred on

his tired horse and made all speed till he was in his office. Within a few minutes he was summoned to the Earl's room.

Dickon made the falcons comfortable and went to drop his bag in the tiny cupboard where he slept behind Master Adam's office. On the pallet he found a suit of the Earl's livery, made to his own size. He was fingering the fine material and trying to realize the import of it when hasty footsteps entered the office and Gareth arrived. He was pale and troubled. He did not immediately ask to see the new hawks.

"There is trouble at Alden, Dickon," he said. " 'Tis Sir Edward."

"Sir *Edward?* Is he not departed for Palestine?" Dickon said in consternation, suddenly aware that he had seen Lentwardine's horse in the distance as they crossed the courtyard.

"Nay, listen!"

Gareth related the surprising story to his friend. Close to the eve of Lentwardine's departure, Sir Tormine de la Saxe revisited the castle. His arrival might have been coincidence, but Gareth believed that it was timed to goad and taunt Sir Edward in his undertaking.

"It was plain to all of us," Gareth said, "that de la Saxe had not forgiven Lentwardine for sparing your life. I feel he made a kind of sport of his gibing, hoping to rouse Sir Edward, as rouse him he did in the end."

"How?" urged Dickon.

"On the face of it," said Gareth, "Sir Tormine pleased all the company as before. At first, we squires noticed very little of what was happening; only Lentwardine seemed moody and kept apart at times. We thought it was the parting and the task ahead that made him thoughtful, but afterwards the pages told us how Sir Tormine plagued him every day more mischievously, making many a jest at his expense. Until one night at supper when he had drunk too much wine, the Fleming tapped Lentwardine on the shoulder as they left the table for bed.

" 'You are a true game hawk,' he said, so loudly that all in the hall could hear. 'But be sure when you face the Turk that you do not take refuge in the nearest monastery instead of meeting him.' "

"What did Sir Edward say?" asked Dickon, horrified.

"He did not speak, but threw his gauntlet at the Fleming's feet," Gareth replied. "And Sir Tormine plucked it from the ground, dazed, like a man who knows he has gone too far. His friends say he was truly ashamed and sorry, and had all the company not been there he would have owned himself wrong. His squires said later he only meant to test our knight, for he had been misled into thinking Lentwardine spent half his time with the priests and was no soldier."

"But they do not fight to the death!" cried Dickon. A fight to the death was something completely foreign to this happy castle and little known in all the district round.

"Indeed they do—a week come Thursday," Gareth said miserably.

"And what does my lord the Earl say?" asked Dickon.

"What is there for him to say? Such a thing has never happened here before," replied Gareth.

But in the evening the Earl of Alden called challenged and challenger to the high table and his anger blazed at them. "I have thought of this matter all night and all day long, and I will have no bloodshed in Castle Alden!" he cried.

"By your leave, my lord, we will fight beyond the castle walls," said Lentwardine briefly, but with reverence.

"This is a tragic matter," continued the Earl, as if Edward had not spoken. "But honor can be assuaged in another fashion. Will you, Sir Tormine de la Saxe, beg pardon of Sir Edward Lentwardine

for words spoken when you were full of wine,
words that no guest could utter in sobriety and
remain our friend?"

"I will, my lord!" replied Sir Tormine with
readiness, and was turning toward Lentwardine
when the younger knight broke in rapidly.

"I cannot grant him pardon, my lord, for the
sake of the honor of my house and Castle Alden,
at whose traditions the Count has not ceased to
mock since he arrived."

The Earl frowned deeply. "Then the matter
shall be decided in a different fashion," he said.
"And in a fashion worthy of this place. I decree
that this matter shall be settled, not by bloodshed,
but by flying Sir Tormine de la Saxe's gerfalcon,
Grettir, and Sir Edward of Lentwardine's Madam
against the heron. If the peregrine shall prove the
better bird, Sir Tormine shall swear to join in
crusade against the Turk. If the gerfalcon tri-
umphs, Sir Edward shall relinquish his Madam
to the Count de la Saxe."

Both men looked up, startled, and met the Earl's
steely gaze, which held them relentlessly. Acceptance was inevitable against so reasoned a justice.
All knew Edward's devotion to his hawk and
guessed he would rather lose his life a dozen times
than surrender Madam to the Flemish Count.

The Earl had not wholly shed his coldness when

Edward waited on him in his private apartments. He sensed the discontent behind the young man's quietness and quenched it with his first remark. "Your life was already pledged to avenge the cause of our Lord in Palestine. What right had you to pledge it elsewhere?"

The young man flushed darkly with humility, and from that moment his resentment died away.

The week that followed was the longest Dickon had ever spent at Castle Alden. Although his new role as squire brought him different duties, he remained, by tacit agreement, Master Adam's apprentice in everything but name, slipping a falconer's smock over his bright uniform and working in the mews as he had done before. Now he had to instruct the newer falconers.

Sir Edward, his departure postponed till after the contest, and the Count de la Saxe spent every available moment in bringing their hawks to an unparalleled perfection. Suspense seized the whole castle and no one thought of anything but the coming Thursday. Squires and pages laid wagers among themselves. Although Madam was favored by everyone, at least half of the castle folk thought she had little chance of beating the great gerfalcon at such a sport as bringing down a heron.

The birds were to fly separately, in itself a risk

to the smaller peregrine, who was used to the help of a mate in stooping on this large and powerful quarry, where not only speed was necessary but the agility to avoid the slashing bill.

The whole of the castle populace was present at the contest, early in the morning of the chosen Thursday. The edge of the great gaunt marshes was crowded with spectators, sworn to keep well behind the scene of action—ladies on horseback, servants on foot, chattering pages, men-at-arms.

To Dickon's delight Sir Edward had asked him to accompany him as falconer squire, even as he had promised months ago. Here they were, riding one behind the other, Lentwardine ahead, with Madam regally astride his gauntlet, Dickon behind carrying the necessary harness.

Abreast of them, at some distance, the Count de la Saxe's party splashed across the tussocks to their agreed position. The fitful morning light shone now and then on the snowy plumage of the beautiful gerfalcon, serene as Madam, so royal and so terrible a rival.

Both birds were at their best, the rumor went round. Did they know this was no joyous hawking party but a deadly battle? Did Madam guess she might be riding her master's fist for the last and final sortie? As the appalling thought struck Dickon, his heart missed a beat.

It was useless to call to mind that at this very

minute the two falconers might have been engaged in deadly battle, thundering down upon
one another in the lists until after a clash of sword
and spurt of blood one would thunder never again.

De la Saxe and his party of friends and attend-
ants were jogging along quietly enough. Between
the two small companies rode the Earl of Alden
and Master Adam, followed by the Earl's page
and a couple of servants leading extra horses.

The weather was perfect for hawking, with
little or no sunshine and a light southwest wind.
Lentwardine's party now halted suddenly, as far
ahead, where the beaters had been carrying out
their duties, a faint shout rose on the air.

De la Saxe's party halted too, but it was Lentwardine whose hand flew to unhood his falcon.
High above their heads and rapidly passing up-
wind, a heron beat the air, so high that the long
legs stretched out behind seemed thin and frail as
reeds.

The Flemish Count, as challenged knight, had
the right to choose the order of his flights and had
decided on the second and fourth, for each falcon
was to be judged on two. Keenly watching the
heron, which passed closer to his party than to
Lentwardine's, de la Saxe must have heard the
triumphant shout with which Edward cast off his
bird.

A moment later the heron suddenly altered

course, and began to ring in circles, climbing higher and higher. It climbed fast, and the young men watching below abandoned their hope that it might be full of fish, and sluggish. The powerful wingbeats carried it up and up above their heads, but even more swiftly flew the peregrine. Now Madam had gained on her prey and was hanging above it. Suddenly the heron seemed to shoot down, down through the clouds, with a small bullet striking the nape of its neck and dropping hundreds of feet below. Before Madam swooped up and then stooped again, the bird had made such distance that Edward's party turned back and galloped up the marsh after the pair of them.

Madam was closer now and found her place more easily. Dickon knew just the moment when her lovely sails snapped-to beside her lithe body and she streamed down upon her prey.

This time the heron dodged even more quickly, but fell toward the ground. Now the trees were close and the heron knew it. It put a final burst of speed into its flight and dived into the shelter of the branches, with Madam so close behind that for a moment they lost sight of her as her sails skimmed over the surface of the water below. Edward's company gasped with disappointment, for it had been a faultless pursuit right up to the end.

Now it was the turn of de la Saxe to fly his hawk. They rode three miles in another direction before a second heron was sighted, and the pursuit led them far beyond the sight of Dickon, left guarding Madam till their return. The castle company swept past him and vanished into the distance. They returned with the news that the gerfalcon had made a mighty capture with great skill, and Lentwardine's face was a mask as Dickon handed him his peregrine.

Over the wild wet wastes they rode, and again a fleeing streak crossed the massed jumble of midday clouds, and Edward unhooded his falcon for the last time.

Dickon would never forget that flight.

For Madam ringing to such a height and at such a pace that they looked vainly for both birds in a streak of light parting two clouds, and then galloped full speed to follow the passage of the duel. Before they could arrive they saw something falling, falling, growing larger and larger as huge wings flapped and folded and flapped again. Before, at a fearful speed, it hit the ground, a small shape detached itself, and followed the landing with a finality that needed no flurry of rising feathers to tell the tale.

The squires watched, from a respectful distance, as the Earl and Master Adam galloped up, followed by the Count de la Saxe. They saw

Madam rewarded with favorite parts of her prize, and then with sweating horses and mud-splashed jerkins they entered on the last contest of the day.

Much later a heron was put up on some far marshes where the going was so difficult that the tired horses stumbled and blew. De la Saxe and his party were newly mounted and so were the Earl and his falconer. Their rapid progress could be well marked by the water splashed up by their horses' hoofs as they galloped. Soon came the repetition of that earlier flight. Reining in their horses, the young men could actually hear the scream of little bells as the gerfalcon tore down the sky. They saw the tumbling, fleeing heron fall out of the heavens with Grettir bound to it by those tremendous talons. They saw both birds falling down, down like plummets. Then they were gone. The sky was empty.

Every face in Lentwardine's party blanched, every man drew in his breath and then let it out in a shout to his horse to gallop. Over the rise they thundered and splashed, and saw the Earl and Master Adam galloping ahead of them.

A quarter of a mile farther on, de la Saxe and his party had arrived and were on the scene, already leaping from their horses. Lentwardine and the squires arrived covered with peat and bog water, to leap calf-deep into the soft green surface of the spit of ground where the drama had ended.

The great gray wings of the heron were still flapping, and as Tormine de la Saxe ran in upon his motionless hawk the heron rose, flapped again, took three or four tottering steps that grew stronger, and then rose in the air.

Among the feathers that were scattered on the green floor of the marsh the gerfalcon lay limp and spread-eagled, with a broken neck. In the startling descent from heaven to earth he had not loosed his grip during that last and most perilous second before landing, and had met death.

The first reaction of the whole company was shock and dismay, for the death of a falcon is tragedy. De la Saxe picked up the body and the rest avoided looking at his face. After a long silence, Lentwardine stepped forward and said a few words to him.

Those listening thought he was praising the bird, for Sir Tormine nodded, fingering over and over again the long, fine, ruthless claws that drooped so limply across his gauntlet. From them two small gray feathers presently detached themselves and fluttered to the ground.

Lentwardine took off his gauntlet and fingered one of the varvels. "Let us each wear one of these, de la Saxe, when we ride against the Turks!" he cried, so boldly that everyone recoiled in dismay, their glances flying to the face of the Flemish knight.

But he, with a bold laugh that rivaled Edward's own, cried, "Ay, Sir Edward! That will we!" And wrenching the silver varvels with his crest and the bird's name engraved on them from the dead bird's leg, he handed one to the younger knight. They rode back together across the wet cold marshes to Castle Alden.

CHAPTER 16

Last Flight

AT LAST THE DAY CAME, POSTPONED ONCE AGAIN while de la Saxe equipped himself and collected his company, for Lentwardine to depart for the Crusades. In his train were many squires who had manned their hawks as boys by Dickon's side.

When the company had clattered away over the castle drawbridge on their perilous journey, armed with the Earl's blessing, Dickon knew that only a passing envy had plucked his heartstrings. His place was with the hawks.

Madam had not gone with Lentwardine. After her epic flight he had decided not to risk her life in battle or in savage and unknown lands. Perhaps, too, he felt he owed this renunciation to the Count de la Saxe, whose courageous acceptance of his own loss, and wholehearted readiness to pay the price of failure and join Edward's Crusade, had won the respect of everyone in the castle.

Whatever Edward's reason, it was probable that only the Earl and his head falconer were fully informed of it. After deep consultation, Master Adam told Dickon that Madam was to be set free. "She shall go out and breed in her own noble pattern before age overtakes her," said the old man. Startled and sad as he was, Dickon could not but approve the decision.

And later that same day he stood with the falcon sitting on his glove, quiet, as if she strained to hear the last echo of the master whose life she had shared so closely.

"Take her forth now and cast her off!" Master Adam told Dickon. Gareth rode with him to the moors.

She was Dickon's first love, this bird, and with her talons on his wrist he rejoiced that he, who had captured her, should be the one to set her free.

They rode through a wood onto the edge of the

wide heath where, long ago, he had dared to test his falconry, and Lentwardine had caught him. Not for sentiment had Dickon chosen this place, but because the wood was near to fall back on if Madam followed them. Quietly, kindly, they must desert her till her own wild instinct took charge, as it surely would.

They tied their horses to the foot of a tree. Gareth helped Dickon to remove the falcon's jesses, gently undoing the familiar knot, unfastening the silver varvels and the Indian bell. They lay lightly in Dickon's hand, small instruments that had played such thrilling music. Still hooded, the falcon stretched her talons wonderingly, missing the weight of her harness.

Gareth and Dickon walked out on the heath.

The pale November sunshine gleamed from behind the clouds, sending shafts of light from heaven to earth. Rain blew up on a southeast wind but passed them by. The sky began to clear above them.

"Now!" said Dickon, and unhooded the free falcon.

The beautiful steely blue body perched on his fist, turning her head from right to left. The breeze stirred the dappled feathers of her breast, and her talons gripped and loosed his gauntlet ready for flight.

It was Gareth who shouted when Dickon cast her off. A thick lump in his throat caught Dickon's breath and made him gasp. When he breathed freely again, she was ringing above them. She climbed in ever-widening circles. From the size of a thrush she dwindled to that of a wren, from a wren to a gnat, and still she mounted.

Like some small pinpoint on a shaft of light the falcon hung, and they prepared to leave her, knowing she would wait an hour or more for the game she expected and watched for.

A gust of wind blew suddenly, and all in a moment her instinct changed. Just as, long months ago she had left her gay young falconer and ridden away on the wind to ultimate disaster in the pine tree, so now a whim seized her in full flight. The small speck hurtled away toward the northwest as if the sense of freedom filled her sails.

"She's gone!" Dickon cried.

They saw her a moment longer; then sun and cloud blotted her out. The falcon had shed her past experience and joined the natural cycle of the years, to make her home, and presently to choose a mate, among the company of noble hawks.

Glossary of Terms

Austringer. One who flies a short-winged hawk.

Bate. Plunge downward from the fist.

Cast. A team of two or three hawks.

Cope. Trim the talons.

Enter a hawk. Fly it at live quarry.

Eyas. A nestling hawk.

Eyrie. A nest.

Falcon. In general, a long-winged hawk—peregrine, gerfalcon, kestrel, etc. In falconry, the name was usually applied to a female bird, the male being called a tiercel.

Falconer. Breeder or trainer of hawks for hunting.

Flight feathers. Longest wing feathers.

Fly at the lure. The hawk is trained to dive onto a bundle of feathers swung on a leash.

Full pitch. The highest point of flight.

Gauntlet. Falconer's glove.

Gerfalcon. Large falcon from the arctic regions.

Goshawk. A short-winged hawk.

Hack pen. Training pen.

Haggard falcon. Wild falcon.

Hawk, long-winged. True falcons, such as peregrine, gerfalcon, kestrel, etc.

Hawk, short-winged. Goshawk, sparrow hawk, etc.

Hood. Put a hood over a hawk's head, hiding the eyes.

Imp. Mend a broken feather.

Imping needles. Needles used in mending feathers.

Jesses. Thongs attached to a hawk's leg.

List. Tournament or contest.

Lure. Bundle of fur or feathers used in training hawks.

Man a hawk. Train a hawk.

Mews. Hawk houses.

Passage hawk. A hawk on migration.

Peregrine. A true falcon.

Rake away. Fly after game.

Rouse, mantle, and *warble.* Gestures used by a hawk signifying readiness to fly.

Sails. Wings.

Sharp set. Hungry.

Stoop. The dive of a falcon on her prey.

Talons. Claws of a bird of prey.

Tiercel. Male falcon.

Tiltyard. Tournament field.

Train. Tail.

Varvels. Small flat rings for a hawk's jess.

Wait on. Balance or hang in the air at a height, waiting for quarry.